LOOKING FOR ADMIRAL FARRAGUT

By CHARLES G. HAUN

TWO SHARP DOGS PUBLISHING

LOOKING FOR ADMIRAL FARRAGUT. Copyright © 2012 by Charles G. Haun. Published by Two Sharp Dogs Publishing, Maryville, Tenn (www.twosharpdogs.com). All rights reserved to the author and publisher, including the right to republish this work in any form.

This book is a work of fiction. Names, characters, places and incidents are products of the author's imagination or are used fictitiously. Any resemblance to actual locales, incidents or persons, living or dead, is coincidental.

PROLOGUE

In December 1797, Jorge Farragut, a Spanish seaman who had fought in the American Revolution, bought 640 acres of heavily wooded land on the border of Indian Territory outside of what is now Knoxville in eastern Tennessee. The place, called Stoney Point, was located on what was then called the Holston River, and Farragut obtained a license to operate a ferry there. In 1801 James Glasgow Farragut was born at Stoney Point to Farragut and his wife, Elizabeth Shine. At about age 8, after his mother's death, the boy was adopted by Commodore David Porter and changed his name to David Glasgow Farragut. Porter secured the young Farragut an appointment as a Midshipman Cadet in the United States Navy, and he saw his first combat action in the War of 1812.

Farragut became the Navy's first rear admiral in 1866 and is best remembered for his cry of "Damn the torpedoes, full speed ahead," which is still an inspiration today. Fighting for the Federal Army in the Civil War, Farragut carved his name into the annals of history and is honored by monuments in New York, Washington, D.C., Spain and elsewhere. In 1900, the Bonny Kate Chapter of the Daughters of the American Revolution, based in Knoxville, Tenn., erected a marble shaft at Farragut's birthplace. Admiral Dewey, fresh from his distinguished performance in the Spanish-American War, was on hand to dedicate the marker, which remained there for 111 years. In 2011, it went missing.

CHAPTER ONE

My wife came to the breakfast island carrying one of the two newspapers she receives each morning.

"Admiral Farragut is missing," she said.

"Yeah, he's missing all right; he's been out of sight since about 1870. The month of August I think, but don't hold me to that."

"No, his monument is missing. It's gone."

"Which monument are you talking about?" I asked.

"The one at Lowe's Ferry, the one you said you played on when you were a boy."

"So how in the flip is a huge block of granite missing?" I asked. The object we were talking about was at least five feet tall and three feet wide. "I know somebody didn't walk off with it."

"The lady that owned the property gave it away," she said, handing me the newspaper.

That monument was there because that was Farragut's birth place. It had been there at least a hundred years.

"I'm checking this out. It can't just disappear," I said.

Well, it did. They sneaked that thing out of there, like a rat against the baseboard.

Of course I was ticked that the monument had been moved. I am an Admiral. No, not a commissioned one like the admiral himself. I'm a Farragut Admiral. Farragut was the name of the school I attended. The Admirals was our nickname.

I was the captain of the Admirals basketball team the year we ended a 42-game losing streak. I played quarterback on the Admirals football team. I sang bass in an all-male choir called the Admiral's Men. I had a poem published in *The Admiral*, the name of our senior yearbook. I also have an anchor tattooed in an inconspicuous spot.

And if that is not enough, I have a vintage photograph of my cousin and me as boys, sitting atop the Admiral Farragut monument at Lowe's Ferry, with a young lady, quite our senior. For the life of me, I don't remember her name, but I do remember that she was wearing a red corduroy jumper and a white sweater. As I said, we were boys, much too young to realize the sacrifices Admiral Farragut made, but old enough to appreciate that white sweater.

I spent some of the best years of my childhood a rock's throw away from that monument. I learned to swim at the Lowe's Ferry boat ramp, a mere 25 feet from the huge stone proclaiming the birth of Admiral David Glasgow Farragut. Being an avid fisherman I often pulled my boat up to the ramp, walked up the slight hill, and paid a visit to the monument.

A couple of weeks after I read the newspaper my wife handed me, my search for the missing monument had been limited to reading newspaper archives and browsing the internet. In searching for that photo of me and my cousin and the monument, I also spent some time going through old photographs my grandfather had left my mother.

It was behind an old framed picture of the monument that I found a letter that intensified the search. I'll give you the gist of the letter. It said that there were 50 gold bricks hidden in the base of the monument. Those bricks at today's gold prices are worth nearly five million dollars. Now if that kind of information fails to get your fire burning, then your wood is wet.

Suddenly I felt the need to step up the search. The newspaper had quoted other "concerned individuals" who wanted it to come home. The Bonny Kate chapter of the DAR, the very chapter that donated the monument in 1900, was highly perturbed, and made no bones about the fact that they wanted it returned. A Folk Life Museum passed an agenda to recover the monument, but at the same time said they would wait to see if the DAR recovered it. Some of my best friends are passive aggressive.

The next several days I spent hours going through every picture, every card, and every scrap of paper in the albums and boxes my mother left me. Never was the monument or the gold mentioned again.

I gave you the gist of the letter. There wasn't really that much more. The letter was signed "Sonny." Its writer stated that he (I presumed it was a he) was being detained in a little town called Rusten, not far from Hutchinson, Kansas. Sonny had met a man who claimed that Jorge Farragut, the father of Admiral David, had somehow put gold in the monument.

Sonny wrote that when his time was up he would be there to help Granddad recover the bounty. The letter was dated June 17, 1956.

I stepped up the search. The newspapers ran my ads. I visited every radio and TV talk show in the local area that would have me, proclaiming to be the savior of the monument. I pleaded for any information, never failing to say, "I'm here for you. I want to help you get the monument back." The public did not respond.

On Tuesday of the next week, I got a call.

"Is this Charlie Grant?" the caller asked.

"That's me," I replied.

"Mr. Grant, this is Ella Knight. I am the director of the entertainment committee for the Stoney Point Chapter of the Daughters of The American Revolution."

"How may I help you?" I asked.

"We would like for you to speak at our next luncheon, which is next Monday. Our chapter regent, Miss Hancock, would love for you to share with us the patriotic reasons you are pursuing Admiral Farragut's monument."

"Miss Hancock?" I asked. "As in ... the Declaration of Independence?"

"Direct lineage, of course," Mrs. Knight said. "She was enthralled to learn of your efforts to recover the monument."

I accepted immediately. Enthralled? I have been around for a few years. I have never had a woman say she was enthralled.

Wednesday I called the out-source line that handles my company's retirement and payroll issues. Finally the music stopped and I was connected to a help aid. The problem was that the woman who answered was on a mountain in Turkey, and spoke Russian with a Spanish accent. Well, that's how it seemed to me. After several attempts to try to and have her figure my retirement, I gave up and went to find my boss. I thought my request to him was reasonable.

"I want to take my five weeks vacation starting next week, and if I should find what I'm looking for, I won't be back."

Then I headed to my aunt's house across the river from me. It's about four miles as the crow flies, but I didn't notice one offering me a ride. I drove the 15 miles on the "new bridge," now 20 years old.

My aunt is 93, hard of hearing, but in good health otherwise, and a mind like a steel trap. I asked her if she remembered anyone kin to Granddad named Sonny.

"Oh Lord, honey, you must be talking about Sonny Brown. He was not kin to any of us. Your dad met him somewhere and got him acquainted with my dad." That made sense. My father, the first Charles Grant, was a friend to everyone, and he probably dragged lots of people home to meet his father-in-law. But as my aunt explained it, this acquaintance had stuck with Granddad.

"Sonny got to where he came to see dad all the time. The last we heard of him he was in jail. I think it was in Kansas. Yes, it was Kansas, I remember now, it was Rusten, Kansas. Dad said he got about five letters from him. They were all postmarked from the jail, and he burned them."

"Did he ever get out of jail?" I asked.

"I just don't know. I guess he did. He never came back to see Dad."

"Was Sonny his real name?"

"No. He had a funny name. Lord, what was his name? Oh, I know," she said. "It was Darwin."

Trying to find a way to fly into Topeka, Kansas is not the easiest task. Information is vague. The on-line site was not much help, and since my patience has usually exhausted itself in less than 10 minutes, I gave up and made flight arrangements the old-fashioned way, by picking up the phone and asking an agent to do it for me. I planned to leave shortly after the DAR luncheon. The sooner I could get this project underway the better. I now had a name and a place, thanks to my aunt, and both name and place needed to be checked out. One thing that was bugging me was the fact that there had been five letters, and my granddad had claimed to have burned them. Of course, I knew he had not burned one of them, and I wondered if he had really burned the rest. I wondered why would he mention them at all?

The Stoney Point Chapter of the Daughters of The American Revolution held their meetings in the basement of the Lakeshore Methodist church. It was a modern structure built on a hill overlooking the lake. The sign in front said, WE DISMISS EARLIER THAN THE BAPTISTS. I parked at the rear and entered the meeting room.

The entertainment director, Mrs. Knight, met me as soon as I came into the room.

"Mr. Grant," she said. She peered at me. "Grant. Any relation?"

"To the canny general who became the president of the United States or to the whiskey-soaked rounder who destroyed the South?"

"Aren't they one and the same man, Mr. Grant?" she asked. I had to give Mrs. Knight credit. Not many people can hold two views of a man.

"Could be," I said. "Call me Charlie."

She introduced me to the ladies assembled, including the nine charter members. East Tennessee, where Admiral Farragut was born, was a Federal stronghold during the Civil War, but in the generations since, the DAR types all appeared to be from old money and southern aristocracy. I was amazed that it did not seem to bother these elderly southern belles that the man whose monument they were interested in saving, while born in the south, had spent a great deal of his time trying to destroy it. I suppose if your father fought in the American Revolution, all is forgiven.

The last lady Mrs. Knight introduced me to was Miss Hancock, the Chapter Regent. I was stunned. She was a willowy wisp of a woman, three days past life support. She looked like a dead woman walking. Only she wasn't walking. She was sitting in the middle of the room in a leather lift chair, her hair and skin the same shade of ghostly pale. Her eyes had a milky skim over them. Somewhere I had heard this only happens to virgins. I took her hand and it felt like a bird claw, and the veins on the back of it stood out like blue rivers on a topography map. I listened to see if she was still breathing.

"It is a pleasure to meet you, thank you for asking me to speak," I said.

"I hope you plan to address this subject fervently," she whispered.

I looked dead on into her cloudy eyes and spoke clearly. "I intend to shell it right down to the cob."

And that is what I did, but first I listened to three eighth grade girls read their essays on why they thought we should keep the "Star Spangled Banner" as our national anthem, and not the song "America the Beautiful." As they were reading, I was sitting at the speakers table with Mrs. Knight, eating my lunch. It consisted of one half of a chunky pimento cheese, and one half of a watercress and cucumber sandwich. Dessert was a thumb-print cookie with lemon icing. The liquid refreshment was the worst raspberry punch I had ever tasted. I looked around for more cookies to try and kill the taste of the watercress, cucumbers, and raspberry, but I guess one per person was the limit.

While the young girls read their essays, I gave some thought to the watercress and cucumbers. I had seen watercress grow in the creek on my Granddad's old farm, just a few feet down from where the cows drank. The cows wouldn't eat them, or at least I never saw them munching on any. The cucumber is not much higher on the food chain, in my opinion. A hog won't even eat a cucumber.

Really, at the risk of sounding chauvinistic, I think we could probably blame all of the green vegetables our mothers forced down our throats on Eve. When she succumbed to temptation in the Garden of Eden, and ate the apple, the food source changed. She and Adam had to leave the garden and hustle up grub on their own. It became necessary for them to eat the herbs of the field. I'm sure watercress and cucumbers were in that mix somewhere.

The applause for the last essay brought me back to reality, and I realized that Mrs. Knight was introducing me as the guest speaker. I had promised Miss Hancock I would shell it down to the cob. Now was the time to put up or shut up. I stood and called the three young girls to the stage, and handed them small American flags to give to the ladies in the room. Get ready, Miss Hancock, I thought; I'm taking the corn out of the basket.

"Again, thank you for having me," I said. "Thank you for giving me a platform to talk about something that means a great deal to me, the missing monument of a great American hero, Admiral David Farragut, born James Glasgow Farragut, just around the corner, more than 100 years ago. The land owner who had the land where the monument had sat for 100-plus years decided to have it removed, and gave it to a collector. They hauled it away, and we don't know how long it had been gone before someone realized it wasn't there."

I paused and took a drink of water to try and kill the taste of the cucumber that kept coming back.

"Don't get me wrong. I'm not blaming the land owner. The reason the monument is missing is apathy. An apathetic society and the cavalier attitude of our political leaders. You have in your possession a small American flag. I gave it to you to call attention to liberty, patriotism, and sacrifice. Suppose your ancestors had taken the offhanded attitude that our society today has taken. You would probably be holding a flag representing a different country."

From there I took the ladies on a journey back through the Revolutionary War. From Concord to Lexington, to the Boston Harbor, and inside the Continental Congress, we traveled. I had them there to hear Patrick Henry say "I only regret that I have but one life to give for my country." The ladies were there when Nathan Hale opted for liberty or death. I gave them every quote and misquote I knew about the Revolutionary War. I even used a story from an old Andy Griffith show about Paul Revere's horse snorting as it ran through the cobbled streets. I had them hanging onto the horse's mane, while riding beside Paul. I also made as many references to John Hancock as I could think of, solely for Miss Hancock.

"So, ladies, would the John Hancocks, the Samuel Adams, the Nathan Hales and Patrick Henrys stand by and watch things they hold dear disappear? I think not. Would our beloved Admiral Farragut stand by for such a travesty? I think not. Finding this monument will be an enormous task. There will be many obstacles. But in the words of our beloved Admiral, whose father fought with your ancestors, 'Damn the torpedoes, full speed ahead.'"

And in the best vocal imitation of a Southern Baptist minister that I could muster, I said, "Ladies, keep standing for the things you stand for. God bless the Daughters of the American Revolution, and God bless America."

I looked over and saw the women gathered around Miss Hancock. I hurried to her chair. She had her eyes closed and a slight smile on her face.

"Is she okay?" I asked.

She opened her eyes. "I'm fine," she whispered. "I just felt a little faint, but at the same time I felt so warm and tingly inside and out."

It dawned on me. I looked into her eyes. They looked clearer. Miss Hancock had taken the ecstasy rollercoaster into the big "O" fairground. She had won the ultimate prize without paying the supreme sacrifice. It was a spinster's dream.

"Was that fervent enough?" I asked.

I turned, squared my shoulders, thrust out my chest, and marched to the door. If you got it, flaunt it.

CHAPTER TWO

Still burping cucumbers, and picking bits and pieces of watercress from between my teeth, I turned east on to I-140 and headed to the airport. I had chosen to fly into Kansas City and from there to Salina. I had no idea what I was going to find, but when you're motivated by gold, you dismiss the unpleasant options. I called my wife from my cell phone and gave her a time to meet me at the airport before I left. After today it could be a while before I saw her again. However, five million dollars can help soothe the pangs of separation anxiety.

There were storm clouds looming in the western sky, but evidently the pilot got routed around them. The flight into Kansas City was smooth and uneventful. I was glad because it gave me time to review the papers and printed matter I had brought with me.

I had been calling the stone a monument, but in every printed article I had, it was being called a marker. I had also thought the stone was granite, but it appeared to be marble. Oh well, a rose by any other name, and you know the rest of the story.

There seemed to have been several attempts to rescue and restore the marker over the years, but they had never gotten out of the planning stages. Several people with great intentions had initiated some action, but each time there was no follow-through. Finally the land owner beat everyone to the punch, and gave the monument, or marker, or whatever it is away.

When the announcement came to button up the trays, fasten seatbelts, and put your seat back in its normal upright position, I had more questions than answers. One thing that puzzled me, yet intrigued me at the same time, was the fact that the DAR was interested in a Civil War marker. The Bonny Kate chapter in Knoxville, Tennessee, a noted and historic group, actually donated the marker I was chasing in 1900. They even had the clout to get Admiral Dewey to dedicate the marker. Which led to another puzzling thing, why would Dewey come back from Manila, just to place a marker? But the real question is why would I go looking for something just because a man named Darwin (Sonny) Brown said it had gold inside of it? I didn't have a reasonable answer for that.

Waiting in airports is not one of my favorite pastimes, but I found a copy of Craig Johnson's book *Hell Is Empty* in the gift shop, and the clock hands moved rapidly. The flight to Salina was smooth and fast. The Salina airport uses an aircraft called the PC-12. It is a Swiss-made turbine, almost like a corporate jet, and I liked it from the time we boarded.

My only problem with the flight was the person sitting next to me. He never shut up from the time we were seated until we stepped off the plane in Salina. The guy was a marvel. He invented the Hubble Telescope, many years before its actual debut. He had a computer rigged up at MIT 30 years before the old punch card types came along. In Germany, when he had vacationed there, he had just happened to visit a Volkswagen plant. They took his advice that the engine should be in the rear. It was his utterance to no one in particular that the car reminded him of a beetle that determined what the car would be called. From shaking hands with MacArthur, upon his return, to sitting with the engineers at Houston when the Eagle landed, this gentleman had done it all.

I'm sure he would have kept on talking but after we got off the plane, I faked an incoming call on my cell. I looked up from my nonexistent phone call and saw him headed toward baggage, talking to some unsuspecting soul. I will say this. The man had to be a freak of nature. I added it up, and if the man had worked all the places he said he did, he would be 172 years old. I swear he didn't look a day past 65.

The car rental agency had bumped me up to a full-size car, and I graciously accepted and set out to find my motel. Before checking in, I found a restaurant just across the street and pulled into its parking lot. It had been a long day, and it seemed like months since the cucumber sandwich at the Lakeside Methodist Church. The waitress came to seat me, and on the way to the booth she had chosen, I passed the man who had bent my ear on the plane. His mouth was moving a mile a minute, and not from chewing his food. It was from talking. He didn't seem to look up as I passed by, but I didn't want to take the chance of getting caught again. I gobbled down the hamburger and baked potato I had ordered, all the time keeping an eye on him. Although it was part of my meal, I opted not to go to the salad bar. It could be a long time before I ate anything green again.

I was told when I called from my motel room a little later that Rusten County's sheriff had gone home for the day. The jailer said that he would return at eight the next morning and that I did not need an appointment to see him. I made sure the jailer knew I would be there when the sheriff got there in the morning. The next call I placed was to my wife. I had called her from the restaurant to let her know that I had reached Salina, but I had rushed the call because of Mr. Talkative.

"Jack called from Texas today. He said he had been in Oklahoma for two weeks on business."

I had been trying to call my friend who lived outside of Sweetwater, Texas, for several days to tell him that I was coming to his state.

"Did you give him my cell phone number?" I asked.

"No, he got off of the phone too quickly. I didn't even have time to ask him how Linda is. I told him that you would call him. He said that he was going to be at home all this week."

We talked on for another 15 minutes, catching up on the day's events. Her last comment was the reason I had trouble sleeping that night.

"I love you," she said.

No, that wasn't what did it. It was the next part: "Don't let the bedbugs bite."

Usually as soon as my head hits the pillow I'm asleep. Not this night. Just as I dosed off it popped into my mind. Bedbugs! Surely this place does not have bedbugs. I closed my eyes again only to have the feeling that they were crawling on me. There would be no going to sleep until I checked. I stripped the sheets off the bed, and got my penlight out of my travel case. I turned the seams of the mattress down and shined the light into every nook and cranny. I flipped the mattress over and checked the other side. Behind the headboard, under the footboard, I checked. Finally I was convinced that bedbugs had not made it to that motel in Salina, Kansas, and I lay down to sleep. However, it was a most fitful sleep. I remember seeing the clock on the bedside radio reading 12:38.

After that came the dream. In the dream Miss Hancock was dancing with the man who was talking to me on the plane. She rose up out of her lift chair and accepted his hand. He was talking as fast as he could to her as he twirled her bony, frail body around the floor. Cymbals were crashing, drums were beating, and huge strobe lights were flashing. A loud cymbal crash brought me out of my sleep and the dream, only to find that outside the motel a fierce storm was raging. I was too tired to care. I pulled the sheet up tight around me and closed my eyes. I did make a mental note to check on-line the combination of pimentos, watercress, cucumbers, lemon icing, and raspberry. I wanted to know if it causes hallucinations.

CHAPTER THREE

Sheriff Randy Bohannon met me at the door when I came in at 8 the next morning. We exchanged introductions and hellos, and then he told me he couldn't stay.

"I know my jailer told you that I could see you this morning, but I've got a little problem I have to attend to first," the sheriff said. "I should be back in about 45 minutes. I'll be glad to talk with you then."

"That's not a problem. I'll hang around here until you get back," I said.

"You had breakfast?" the sheriff asked.

"Not yet."

"Well, sitting catty-cornered from here is Jack's Diner. The food is good. The waitress can be a pain in the butt when she's cross-threaded, but she won't bite. Hop on over there and grab you a bite to eat, and then meet me back here." I waited until he left the building and then I headed out to the diner.

There were four or five men sitting on stools at a bar drinking coffee and talking. I picked out a table toward the back and sat down facing the door. The waitress showed up with a coffee cup, a coffee pot, and a menu. She poured me a cup of coffee, and dropped the menu on the table. As of yet she had not spoken, and neither had I.

"You know what you want?" she asked.

"I'll have the breakfast special," I said.

She picked up the menu and walked back toward the kitchen. She was a big-boned woman with dyed yellow hair. Her makeup was plastered on to hide lines that probably had shown up because of her having to get up this early every day to serve the public. I would just play it by ear.

I picked up my coffee cup and took a small sip, testing it to see if it was hot. It was awful. That was not coffee in that cup. Like making love in canoe, it was near water. Plus, it had the worst taste. Even worse than the raspberry punch I had yesterday. I wondered how these people were getting that stuff down. I pushed it aside and in a few minutes she was back with the breakfast special, one scrambled egg, two pancakes, and a strip of bacon.

It was good. I just wished I had something to help wash it down with. I noticed that she had not offered water when she brought the coffee. I finished the food, choked it down the best I could, and saw her returning with a coffee pot, I assumed to pour me a refill.

"Something wrong with that coffee?" she asked.

"I just didn't want it," I answered.

"Why?"

"Well, to tell you the truth," I said, "It really doesn't taste good."

"Okay, renowned coffee drinker, what did it taste like?" she asked. I started to see what the sheriff meant by "cross-threaded."

"I don't know, it really didn't have a taste," I lied.

She had the attention of everyone in the diner now and she was going to play for all it was worth.

"You look like a smart man," she said. "Surely you can come up with words to describe what it tastes like."

"Horse piss," I said." It tastes like horse piss."

"So you are a regular horse-piss drinker?" she asked. Timing it to make sure everyone in the diner heard and laughed.

"No," I answered, "But I'd drink of gallon of it before I'd take a sip of that crap you call coffee."

She was undaunted. "Really, can't you be more imaginative than that?"

I dropped a ten spot on the table to cover the breakfast special and the equine bodily fluid in question, and walked toward the door. Then I stopped and turned around.

"How about horse piss with the foam farted off? Does that broaden the spectrum? Does that offer a more picturesque setting?"

I left before she had a comeback. I guessed I wouldn't be eating lunch there.

Randy Bohannon fit my description of how a sheriff should look. He was a tall, rangy fellow with a weathered face and a gray moustache. He had on denim pants and a dungaree shirt. His boots were shined to see your reflection to perfection, and he was wearing a You Roll it by Bailey straw cowboy hat.

I was sitting in the front waiting room of the jail when he returned. He hung his hat on a rack, picked up two coffee cups and motioned me to follow him. We went to a room that was serving as a break and lunch area and he handed me a cup. I filled it with some good-smelling coffee and followed him back to his office.

"Thought you might want a real cup of coffee after visiting Jack's Diner," he said.

"That was some bad stuff. I don't know how anybody drinks it," I said.

"It's been like that for 20 years. People complain, but Linda keeps on making it bad," the sheriff said.

"She was unhappy with me because I didn't drink mine, but I guess she'll get over it."

"She finds somebody to fight with most every day," he said. "If she can't, she just yells at Jack."

"Are they married?" I asked.

"No, they're brother and sister. Neither of them is married. Jack lives in an apartment above the restaurant, and Linda still lives with their mother. They have some real knock-down drag-outs sometimes, but so far they haven't killed each other. I've been called over there twice in the last five years to separate them."

"Maybe you should have put her in jail for a couple of days, and let Jack make the coffee," I said.

He offered me another cup of his but I refused.

"Now how can I help you?" he asked. "I know you told me you were from Tennessee, but what brings you to Rusten, Kansas?"

"I'm trying to find some information on a man named Darwin Brown. He went by the name of Sonny. He was a friend or at least an acquaintance of my grandfather. I found a letter he had sent my grandfather in 1956. The letter said that Mr. Brown spent a stretch in the Rusten jail. My aunt remembered him, but she didn't know what happened to him. I didn't expect to find anyone here that remembered him, but I thought there might be some files or paperwork that mentions him."

"Well. Not only is there probably no one around that remembers him, there's no paperwork either. We lost everything in the big tornado that roared through here in 1976. It blew the jail and the courthouse away. You might have got some of the papers up there in Tennessee. They did find some in Arkansas. It took out everything in the town here but the First Baptist Church, and Millers Ice Company, over there next to the creek."

"Anybody hurt or killed?" I asked.

"We had some people banged up, but nobody killed, thank goodness. I was not the sheriff then, my dad was. He retired that year, and I got appointed to serve out his term to election time. Then I got elected, and have been elected ever since."

He paused, took a long sip of his coffee, and continued his story.

"The funny thing about that day was that my dad had arrested a man named Paul West for drunk and disorderly conduct, and urinating in the street. West owned a junk yard about a mile down the road from here, and if that old man was sober, he was a pretty fair shade-tree mechanic. The problem was he hadn't had a bath in who knows how long, and he stunk like high heaven. My dad had gone to find a water hose to hose him down with when the tornado hit.

"My dad pulled the patrol car in behind the First Baptist Church and never received a scratch. When it blew down the jail here it rolled his deputy across the street like a bowling ball. Broke his collarbone, and cut him up something terrible. Paul West got blown into the creek that runs through here. He was pinned there on the bank until the storm was over. It had ripped all his clothes off except his shoes. The rain had hit him so hard it had nearly blistered his skin. He was as pink as a salmon. I say it was the first time he'd been in water in 20 years. My dad called it Divine Intervention."

"The Lord does work in mysterious ways," I said.

I ended up telling the sheriff the whole story about the chasing the marker. All but the part about the gold, that is. I kept that part to myself. I told him that I had wanted to stop in Rusten to see if there was anything I could find about Darwin Brown being in jail there, and then I intended to fly to Dallas, and put the word out that I was looking for the marker.

"You don't have Sonny Brown, but do you have anything in your files on any Darwin Browns in this town?" I asked.

The sheriff drew his chair closer to his desk, and opened the database in his computer. For a few minutes we were quiet while he searched.

"Bingo," he said. "I don't have anyone in my town, but just outside of Hutchinson lives a man by the name of Darwin Brown III. He got a speeding ticket last week and he hasn't paid it yet."

"That has to be his grandson," I said. "Can you give me the address?"

He found his pen and wrote down the address and phone number, and handed it to me.

"Don't tell him or anyone else that I gave you this," he said.

I called the number from the sheriff's office and Mr. Brown answered. I told him who I was and what I was there for and he agreed right away to see me. I waited while he gave me the address, pretending to write it down. I said goodbye to the sheriff and thanked him for his help. I plugged the address into the rental car's GPS and headed out to meet Mr. Darwin Brown. The fact that Darwin Brown had gotten a ticket was on my mind and probably kept me from getting one. I was actually doing two miles under the speed limit when I passed the patrolman sitting in his car, which was hidden back off the road. If I had had a cowboy hat like the sheriff wore, I would have tipped it at him.

I don't know what I was expecting from Darwin Brown III, but never in all my time have I met anyone as meek, cowed-down, and hen-pecked as he was. The man was the poster child for timidity. He was sitting on his front porch when I pulled into the drive of the modest home. We shook hands and he offered me a seat.

"I hope it's okay if we sit out here on the porch," he said. "My wife is cleaning, and she can't stand having anyone underfoot."

"This is fine," I replied. "It's a nice day for sitting outside anyway."

"I would offer you something to drink, but like I said she would be upset if I tracked in."

"No problem," I said.

Without giving him any details about where I thought the marker was, I filled him in on what constituted my search. I told him about the letter I had found from his granddad to my granddad.

"My aunt said that there were five letters but I only found one."

"I'm sure there were five," Darwin Brown said.

He kept his head down when he spoke, and his voice was really low. I had to lean in toward him with my good ear to hear.

"My granddad was obsessed with gold," Brown continued. "He was looking for every speck he could find. I know the time I spent with him as a boy, he was always talking about gold."

"How did your granddad know about the gold in the marker?" I asked.

Before he could answer his wife stepped out onto the porch. She was a medium-sized woman with permanent frown lines. Her face would have cracked like a dried-up lake bed if she had even entertained the thought of smiling. Here was a woman that was reveling in her misery. The dress she had on was way too young for her, and besides she didn't have the legs or the figure the dress needed to accentuate the positive.

"Jasper is on his way over here," she said. "We're going shopping for him another truck. It's a shame he has to drive that piece of junk he's driving now. Remember I want you to paint that utility room. You're wasting your time talking about that gold. There never was any gold. If there was gold, I hope you'd have had the good sense to find it. Then maybe we wouldn't have to live like second-class citizens. We're going to eat while we're out, so you'll have to fix you something. I'm not going to shop for Jasper a truck all day, and come home and cook."

She let the storm door bang as she went back inside. Darwin had kept his head down the entire time she was talking, and finally he raised it, after making sure she wasn't there any longer.

"Where was I?" he asked.

"You were going to tell me how your granddad knew there was gold in the marker," I said.

"Oh yeah, well in 1956 he was in jail for most of the whole year. It was the jail over in Rusten, because that's where they lived then. He met a man while he was in there that claimed to have ancestors that sailed with Jorge Farragut. Farragut was called Mesquida then or something that sounded like mosquito. I'm trying to recall exactly the way my daddy told it. Anyway, Farragut and this man's kin were in the Spanish merchant marines together. The man's ancestor actually served under Farragut for a while. He claimed that they took all kinds of gold and that Farragut hid a lot of it in different places. He always claimed to my granddad that his ancestors said that Jorge Farragut was a soldier of fortune. He said that's why Farragut left Spain and joined the United States Navy."

"If you don't mind my asking, why was your granddad in jail?"

Just at that moment a loud diesel engine truck with dented fenders pulled up in the driveway behind my rental car.

"Hold that thought until later, if you wouldn't mind," Brown said, barely audible over the sound of the truck motor.

I consider myself to be an excellent judge of character. Jasper Brown didn't have any. He was about the biggest classless act I had seen in a while. I disliked him from the moment he stepped up on the porch. There was no resemblance to the mild-mannered Darwin the third. Jasper had the face of a jackal, and the eyes of a chicken-killing, egg-sucking dog. There was no way this guy could be trusted. He was wearing a full camouflage outfit with pants, shirt, and shoes of camouflage design. He topped it by wearing a camouflage hat.

"Mama said that you're the man hunting for the gold in that rock."

I didn't answer.

"If you find any gold in that rock then half of it is ours," he said.

"How did you come to that conclusion?" I asked.

"Well, you wouldn't even have known it was in there if it hadn't been for my great-granddaddy."

"I don't know if it's in there now. I don't even know where the marker is," I said.

"I've said all I'm going say. If you find that gold and don't contact me then I'll see you in court. Or better yet, I'll come looking for you."

"You might want to bring the Kansas National Guard with you, if you decide to hunt me down. I don't like threats," I said.

The storm door slammed when he went into the house.

"Is that little prick always that friendly this early in the morning?" I asked.

"This is one of his good days," Darwin Brown whispered.

"Is he in the Reserves or the National Guard?" I asked.

"No, that's just the way he and his friends like to dress."

Darwin's wife and Jasper came out of the house in about 10 minutes. She paused at the end of the porch.

"I want that room painted before I get back. The paint and brushes are in the room. Mister, you are going to have to finish your business with Darwin and hit the road. He's got work to do."

Jasper's truck made as much noise leaving as it did arriving. Darwin waited until it was out of sight before he spoke.

"Granddad was in jail for public endangerment, disturbing the peace, inciting a riot, and every other thing they could think of to keep him in there. It started over water rights. In 1956, the Kansas Water Rights Board made a huge number of changes. The owner of the land that someone wanted to dig a well on had to file an application. Granddad's irrigation well collapsed, and he filed an application to dig another one 20 feet from where the one collapsed. Well, one of the chief engineers that could grant that approval was the son of a man who hated Granddad's father. This feud had been going on for years, I'm told. He just kept sitting on the application until the deadline ran out."

"So your granddad took matters into his hands, I presume."

"He did at that," Darwin the third said. "They were supposed to hear his case at a city council meeting, but the chief engineer used his clout to get it postponed. Granddad was a big gun collector, so he picked out one of his favorite Colt 45s and shot all of the windows, and all of the lights out of the building. He didn't shoot anyone, thank goodness, but he scared everybody to death. He served 10 months because they wouldn't accept his bail.

"My grandmother visited him about a month before he got out, and everything appeared okay. But she left that day and he never saw her again. None of us ever saw her again. She had sold everything on the farm, I guess, just trying to survive. He took it all in stride. He boarded up the house and hit the road with the guy he met in jail. I reckon they went to find gold. He came back after a few years and married a woman whose husband had died and lived out some very good years on his farm. My granddad was an educated man, but he was also down to earth. He was a good man."

I could tell that he meant it.

"Do you believe there is any gold?" I asked him.

"I know there is," he said. "My granddad and that fellow found at least one buried treasure, and probably found more. Having that gold is how my granddad survived and kept that farm going with not enough water to water the crops. He spent a little of that gold along and no one was the wiser. He showed it to my daddy and that's how he made it along, too. Now I'm the only one that knows where it is. If my granddad said there was gold there, then there's gold there."

"Why did he never show up in Tennessee to help my granddad find the gold he said was there?"

"I don't know the answer to that. Maybe he told your granddad why in the letters, but I really don't know."

I shook his hand and thanked him for his time and his honesty.

"I am going to drive to Topeka in the morning, and then catch a flight to Dallas-Fort Worth and from there to Abilene. Let me give you my cell phone number. If you come up with anything give me a call. I going to see a friend of mine in Texas and then get back home."

"Let me give you some free advice," he said, "Watch Jasper. He's a snake and he's mean. He'll hurt you if he can."

"Let me give you some free advice," I said. "Grow a set, grab Jasper up, and take him somewhere for a DNA test. When you determine what I'm pretty sure you already know, kick his and that witchy woman's ass to the curb, and take that gold and get out of here."

"I've been giving that some thought," he said.

CHAPTER FOUR

The Rusten city limit sign came into view and I made a quick decision. I was going to eat a late lunch or an early dinner at Jack's Diner. I don't know if I was in the mood for a fight, or just wanted a greasy hamburger, but I was about to meet up with Linda the waitress from hell again.

As I pulled into the parking lot, Sheriff Randy Bohannon drove in at the same time. He got out of his vehicle first and waited for me to catch up with him.

"Did you come back for some more bad coffee or more abuse?" he asked.

"I don't know what made me stop here," I answered.

The sheriff seated himself at what I assumed was his regular table and I took the chair across from him. In less than a minute Linda arrived.

"Oh, the horse piss drinker has returned," she said.

"I'd like to apologize for that," I replied.

"Don't apologize," she said. "It only shows weakness of character."

"At any rate, I'm sorry for that comment," I told her.

We both ordered the chicken strip basket with honey mustard. The sheriff ordered a coke and I chose lemon with water.

"What was that all about?" he asked, when Linda left to turn in the order.

"I told her the coffee tasted like horse piss, when I was in here before. I guess I left that out when I was telling you about it," I said.

"I think you might have left out more than that," he said. "I kind of got a feeling that you weren't telling me everything."

"Actually I only left out one thing," I told the sheriff. "In the letter that my granddad received from Darwin Brown, it stated that there was gold hidden in the Farragut monument. At today's prices it's about five million dollars worth of gold."

"Do you believe the gold is there?" asked the sheriff.

"I don't anymore," I answered. "I don't know what I was thinking. The gold couldn't be in the monument for several reasons, but the biggest one being that the monument, or marker, is solid marble. Another big one is that Jorge Farragut wasn't there when the monument was. He was living in New Orleans in 1808. The best I can figure he left Stoney Point around 1807 and the monument showed up in 1900."

"So Darwin Brown's letter had false information," Sheriff Bohannon said.

I fanned the gnats off the lemon wedges and squeezed the juice from three pieces into my water. I dropped the slices into the water and added two packets of Sweet & Low. Redneck, high-tech lemonade goes well with chicken strips, and I stirred it swiftly before I answered.

"That piece of information was wrong about the monument," I said. "But, I think that Darwin Brown really believed that there was gold associated with it, and I know that Darwin Brown III believes exactly what his grandfather did."

While we ate I told the sheriff everything about my visit to see Darwin Brown III. The only part I omitted was about the gold that Darwin Brown's grandfather had found after he left the jail. I told him what a shiftless character Jasper Brown was, and how the mother and the son ruled the old man. I told him I expected some kind of trouble from Jasper Brown but wasn't sure what it would be.

Linda came back to our table carrying two pieces of cherry pie with a scoop of ice cream on top of each. She slid one piece in front of the sheriff and gave me the other.

"These are on the house," she said. "It's as close as I get to kissing and making up."

The sheriff's glare at me kept me from saying, "Thank God." Instead I said, "Thank you."

It was clear to me that if I added anything else I was going to be looking down the barrel of whatever kind of pistol the sheriff was carrying. I ate my pie and ice cream in silence.

Traffic was light as I backtracked from Salina to Topeka to get a flight to Texas. My initial plan had been to lie over in Dallas and see what interest I could stir up about the monument. All I knew was that the monument went to Texas. I had no clues to where in Texas. It would have been like looking for a needle in a haystack. I was having a hard time talking myself out of cancelling that trip and heading home. No matter what I had told Miss Hancock and her friends, I had to admit that I started to lose interest in the monument once I realized there was no gold hidden inside. At least I ought to be able to say that I had gone, even if all I did was go say hi to my old friend, Jack, in Sweetwater and then head back home.

Two hours later I was on an American Eagle flight to Dallas. At dinner time I had made it to Abilene. The motel was less than five miles from the airport so I took a cab. I knew that there was a restaurant across the parking lot from the motel, and that's where I was going to eat dinner. Doing it this way, I reasoned, would save me one day on the rental car fee. In the morning I would take a cab back to the motel, rent a car and go see my friend Jack Winston. I had called him from Dallas while I was waiting on my next flight and he gave me the address to his office. He said he would be at work in the morning but would take the afternoon off. After he had left the Navy, he went back to Texas and got a job as a deputy. He was now a detective and loved his work.

Jack Winston and I met for the first time on a train headed to Chicago. We were headed for basic training at Great Lakes, Illinois. We had gone through basic together, got assigned to shore duty at the same place and after shore duty we received orders to go aboard a destroyer in Norfolk, Virginia. We had managed to spend our entire hitch at the same places. That was something almost unheard of, unless you joined the navy on the buddy plan. We had become best of friends. He had moved his wife, Linda, to an apartment about the same time I did when we were assigned to shore duty. Our wives had also become good friends, and down through the years we had kept in touch, although we had talked more infrequently as he had gotten so busy. It had been awhile since our paths had crossed and it would be good to see him again.

"What did you say you were doing that brought you to Texas?" he asked over the phone.

"I'm looking for gold," I said.

"All the gold's in California," Jack said.

"Who are you, the front man for Larry Gatlin?" I asked.

On the other end of the line I just heard blank silence. Sometimes your best material is wasted.

CHAPTER FIVE

After a continental breakfast I called a cab to take me back to the airport to rent a car. I accepted a mid-size and waited until they brought it up from the service area. The customer representative told me that the car had just been washed and serviced and was ready to go. I drove it maybe 12 miles before it stalled, died, wouldn't go anymore. The oil light came on just as it made a loud groan and chugged to a stop. I called the representative and told him I was broken down and told him where I was.

"What happened to it?" the representative wanted to know.

"I have no idea," I answered. "The oil light came on and it stopped."

"Was there any indication that it was running bad before it stopped?" he asked.

"No, look, I don't know anything about cars. I can play the radio and that's about it. Let me give you my best animal analogy. The motor seized up like a horse with twisted intestines, and it quit like a steer in the road. It's already hot out here – send somebody to get me."

It was hotter inside the car than it was standing outside in the sun. About 50 yards off the side of the road there was a small barn and next to the barn were a couple of mesquite trees, or at least that's what I thought they were. The shade of those trees looked really inviting, but I knew I was close to Sweetwater, and that's where the big rattlesnake roundup is every year. I could envision a rattlesnake under every bush between the road and those mesquite trees. I had never been to a rattlesnake roundup, but I had seen pictures of 3,000 snakes in a holding pen at one time. That led me to believe there had to be one or two out there in the bushes. So I was left to pick my poison. I could die of sunstroke or try for the shade and get nailed by a huge rattler. I opted for the sunstroke.

The car was visible long before it reached where I was standing. When it got close I realized that the windows were tinted and there was no way to see inside. The car slowed when it got to where I was and I assumed it was going to stop. However, the car did not stop, and continued on. About a quarter of a mile from me, the car did a U-turn and headed back my way. Once again when it got to where I was standing it slowed to a crawl, but then it sped away at a high rate of speed. Just at that moment I saw the tow truck approaching. I don't know what the driver of the car had in mind, but it didn't give me a good feeling.

Bill Knox was the tow truck driver's name. Actually it wasn't a tow truck; it was a car hauler. He pulled past the broken-down car and then backed up close. He got out of the truck and introduced himself. He was wearing jeans, cowboy boots, and a T-shirt that said "Armadillos are just possums on the half shell."

"Jump in the cab there where it's cool," Bill said. "There's water in that cooler sitting on the console. I'll get this thing loaded and we'll be out of here in a minute."

Air conditioning had never felt so good, and water had never tasted so good. I was burning up. A few more minutes of being in that heat, and I think I would have reversed my decision, and went for the shade, snakes or not. I noticed next to the cooler there was a pistol inside a holster. I wrote it off as being Texas. I had the air conditioning fan on high and was feeling better by the time Bill Knox loaded the car and came back to the driver's side of the truck.

"Were you about to melt down out there?" he asked.

"I was getting a little warm. Thanks for the water. I wanted to go over there to those trees, but I was afraid I might run into a few snakes."

"Yeah, there's probably a few out there, but it may be too hot for them. Didn't anybody offer to help you?" he asked.

"Only one car came by, and it didn't stop. It slowed down, and then went down the road and turned around and came back, and slowed down again. The windows were tinted so I couldn't see who was in it."

"Yeah, I passed that car. Strange that whoever was in it wouldn't help you. People around here are usually more hospitable than that," Knox said.

"You found me pretty quickly," I said. "The rental company must have you on contract."

"We do their repair, engine, and body work. We'll have to do this one, because the guy at the rental place said that after they did the oil change, the mechanic left the oil plug out."

"That explains why it quit," I said. "They don't run very far without oil."

"No, they don't," Knox answered. "Where were you headed?"

"I was on my way to Sweetwater to see an old friend of mine."

"Are you out here on vacation?" he asked.

"No, not really," I replied. The threat of sunstroke had made me chattier than I might have been otherwise. "Actually I came here looking for something. I meant to come here to find a monument or a marker, but I decided I wasn't interested in it after all. I already had the plane fare bought so I just thought I would visit my friend and go home tomorrow."

"What kind of monument were you looking for?" Knox asked.

"It was a marker of Admiral David Farragut. I grew up around it when I was a kid, and somebody said it got moved to Texas. It's a long story."

"Well, you were only about 30 miles from it," he said.

"How do you figure that?" I asked.

"I unloaded it off the truck up there next to Sweetwater Lake. They came by the shop with some carburetor problems, and while they were there they wanted to know if we knew of anyone that could unload the rock. We have all kinds of equipment, so I followed them up there and took it off the truck. Man, you must be living right. In a state as big as Texas you show up 30 miles from where the monument is."

The only thing that came to mind was, "I promised Miss Hancock I'd find it."

"What?" he asked.

"It must be the heat," I said.

We went back to his shop and he unloaded the car from the car hauler. We then got into his personal truck and he took me to the rental car company and I got my refund. I didn't rent another car, because Knox said that he would drive me to Sweetwater Lake to where he had unloaded the monument.

It turned out that he had owned the shop but two years ago handed it over to his son. His wife had died of cancer four years earlier, and now he lived alone. He hung out at the shop with his son sometimes and helped out.

On the way to the site where he unloaded the monument I told him the whole story about what had brought me to Texas. I included the part about going to Kansas to check out the letter about the gold, and why I had decided that there was no gold in the monument. I gave him the low down on Darwin Brown and his son Jasper.

"This Jasper Brown is a strange dude," I told him. "He appeared to me to need an anger management course. He threatened me the first crack out of the box. He told me that if I found the gold, half of it was his. He had on a complete camouflage outfit. Personally, I think he's a couple sandwiches short of a picnic."

"I'm free to travel," he said. "If you want any help hunting that gold let me know."

"I think if I could find the other letters," I said, "they would lead me to where the gold is."

"Don't look now," Knox said, glancing into the rear-view mirror, "But I think we are being followed. It looks like that same car that passed me when I was coming to find you, the one with the tinted windows."

"You really think it's following us?" I asked.

"Yeah, I do. It's been hanging back there for a while. We'll just wait and see what happens when we turn up the road toward the lake."

When we made the turn toward Sweetwater Lake the car followed, but as we got closer to the lake it dropped of sight.

"I could have been wrong," Knox said. "But I don't think so. I'd bet a dollar against a doughnut that we see that car again."

The marker was at a place called Anita's Collectibles. It was a two-story frame house painted white with green trim. The lawn was lush and neatly manicured, and the flower gardens were well attended. There was a fountain next to the front porch of the house, and a professionally edged walk leading to the marker of Admiral Farragut. The concrete still had that fresh uncured look, and the marker had been placed on a mound to make reading the front of it easier. A new, shiny fence enclosed the property, and hours of operation were posted on a painted sign attached to the gate of the fence. We were just pulling into a sizeable, unpaved parking area when my cell phone rang. It was Darwin Brown III.

I had to ask him to speak up. He said that he was in the hospital. Jasper had come back from looking at trucks and beat him up. In his most apologetic voice he told me that he told Jasper where I was going. Jasper and a friend of his had left that very night for Abilene. It was 500-mile drive, but with me not leaving until the next day, it gave them time to get there before I did. Darwin just kept apologizing but I told him to forget it. The person I was mad at was me. I should have never told him where I was going. I hung up the phone and turned back to Bill Knox.

"The mystery of the car following us has been solved," I said. "It looks like it is probably Jasper Brown. He beat his father up and headed out to Abilene to find me."

"Do you expect him to cause trouble?" Knox asked.

"I suppose," I answered. "I don't know exactly what to expect. I guess I'll see how it plays out when he gets here.

"Are you worried about it?"

"Not really worried, just apprehensive. I'll deal with it when the time comes. As my dear old sainted dyslexic mother use to say, we all have our bear to cross."

Anita Walsh was the woman who owned the business, and I could immediately see why Bill Knox was so eager to detour back to her place. She came out of the house when she saw me shooting pictures of the monument with my camera phone. Actually, I think she came out to see Bill Knox. She sure acted happy to see him again, and it was obvious that he felt the same way.

"Well, what brings you back up this way, Mr. Knox?" asked Anita Walsh.

"Please, call me Bill. I brought this gentleman up here to see this monument," Knox said.

"Oh, you're interested in the monument?" she asked, finally taking her eyes off Knox and looking at me.

"I was until about a day ago. I grew up where this monument was, and played on and around it when I was a kid."

"I'm glad you are no longer interested in it, because it is the one thing that I have here that is not for sale. I just hope you're not representing anyone," she said.

"No, I'm not working for, or representing anyone. I mean, I talked to some people about why I wanted to find it, but I guess I sort of lost interest."

"And the pictures?" Anita asked.

"I may show them, but I promise you I will never disclose where the monument is located."

"I would appreciate that," she said. "I understand there have been some upset people over the fact that the monument got moved."

"There were some people pretty hot about it," I said. "The most, I guess, is the DAR chapter that donated it. But really I expect in a little while that everything will calm down, and most people will forget about it."

"Well, the offer was made to me that I could have it if I could get it moved. I think it is a great collectible, so I had it hauled down here." She hesitated. "Bill unloaded it for me, and he has agreed to come back and move it if I decide on a different location."

I put my cell phone back in my pocket and moved toward the gate.

"Would you gentlemen like a glass of lemonade?" Anita asked.

Before we could accept or decline the offer, the car with tinted windows pulled into the parking lot. Jasper Brown got out of the passenger side waving a gun.

"Run, go call 911," I said to Anita Walsh.

Bill Knox and I moved toward the parking lot where we met Jasper Brown.

"I told you I would track you down," he said waving the gun. "I told you I expected half of that gold. It's mine. My great-granddaddy found out where it was. Now I want it."

"There's no gold," I said.

"Don't lie to me," he yelled. He pushed the gun into my face. "Now tell me where it is."

"Put that gun down, you idiot," Knox said, as he reached for it.

Jasper Brown spun and put the gun in Knox's face. "You go get in your truck or I will shoot both of you. You don't have anything in this. Now go. I'm not kidding."

From the look in Jasper Brown's eyes I didn't think he was kidding. This guy was crazy or so doped up he didn't know what he was doing. He watched until Knox got into his truck and turned back to me.

"Now where is the gold?" Jasper asked.

"I told you. There is no gold. Not in that monument. That is a solid piece of marble. There is no way anybody could hide anything in that rock."

"I'm not going to argue anymore," Jasper said. "Come on. Go get in my car. I'm going to take you away from this place, and I'm going to kill you for stealing from me and lying to me."

He put the gun into my back and pushed me toward his car. Bill Knox stepped out of the truck, but stayed behind the door.

"Let him go right now," Bill said.

Without any warning Jasper turned and fired two shots at Bill. Both shots hit the fender of Bill's truck. The next shot came from Bill. He stepped out from behind the truck door and fired. The bullet hit Jasper in his right shoulder, the gun fell from his hand, and he went down. I immediately grabbed the gun. I knew Bill had the pistol in the car hauler, but I didn't know he had put it in his truck. At that moment a skinny young man stepped out of the driver's side of the car with his hands up.

"Don't shoot," he yelled. "I don't have a gun."

"Get over there next to where your buddy is," Bill said.

The young man moved over next to where Jasper Brown lay.

"How bad is he bleeding?" Bill asked.

"I don't know," the young man said. "I don't see much blood."

"Tear away his shirt and make a bandage," Bill said.

The young man did as he was told. He tore strips from Jasper Brown's shirt, and used them to bandage the wound the best he could. Jasper Brown lay there as if he was in shock. He wasn't moving at all. In his eyes I could see nothing but hate, but he never opened his mouth.

"Listen," the young man said. "I didn't have any part in this. He held a gun on me all the way from Rusten, Kansas. We drove over 500 miles last night with him yelling and waving that gun. He swore he'd kill me if I didn't help him."

"Are you a friend of his?" I asked.

"We're cousins. He came over to my apartment and made me take my car because the windows were tinted. He said that we were going to Abilene, Texas, because that's where you were going. We watched you get off the airplane in Abilene, and we just started following you. He's crazy and he's mean. He's got drugs in my car. He's been taking them all night."

I turned back around to Bill Knox.

"What kind of trouble are you in for shooting him?" I asked.

"None, it was self defense," Bill said. "The guy tried to kill me. I have a carry permit for this gun. It's legal. I've never shot a person before. In fact I've never shot anything but targets. I am accurate though. If I had wanted to kill him I could have. I hit exactly where I aimed. I'll place some heavy money on the fact that the gun he has is not legal."

In the distance we could hear sirens. I was still shaking. I had nearly died in Sweetwater, Texas, all for the want of a few gold bars. As Virgil, the ancient Roman poet said, "Curst greed of gold, what crimes thy tyrant power had caused," or something like that.

Texas law enforcement rolled in like an early morning fog. Anita Walsh's parking lot was filled with cars. A Texas Highway Patrol had joined the caravan. Along with the ambulance and EMTs, there were several county mounties, the sheriff was there, and my old friend Jack Winston had made the trip. I had a fleeting thought: I'll bet Anita Walsh wished, for this one day at least, that she owned a doughnut shop.

Jasper Brown had not said a word since he had been shot. Just as soon as he saw all the law enforcement he started yelling.

"They robbed me. That's why I did this. They were stealing my gold."

Jack Winston looked at me, all business.

"What's he talking about?" he asked.

"He thinks that there is gold in that monument up there," I said, pointing toward the rock.

"There is gold in there," Jasper Brown yelled. "He knows that. He's trying to act like it's not in there. My great-grandfather told his grandfather it was there. I have as much right to it as he does. He's stealing it."

"At one time I thought there might be gold in that monument, too," I told Jack Winston and the rest of the officers that had gathered around. "But now I don't."

"Why don't you tell us the whole story?" Jack Winston asked.

I waited for the EMTs to get Jasper Brown loaded and hauled off to the ambulance before I told the story. They placed an oxygen mask over his face before they carried him away, and I'm sure it was more to shut him up than it was to aid his breathing.

"This may take a minute or two," I said. "That monument sitting right over there use to be in my home town. I found out not too many days ago that it had been moved to Texas. At the time I didn't know where in Texas. I found a letter in some old pictures my granddad left my mother that suggested that there was gold hidden in that monument. The letter was addressed to my granddad, and it was from Jasper Brown's great-grandfather."

One of the deputies said, "You mean that man they just put into the ambulance?"

"Yeah, that one," I said. "Anyway to make a long story short, I found a man named Darwin Brown outside of Hutchinson, Kansas." I explained that it was his grandfather who had sent my grandfather the letter while he was in jail, and how he had been in with a man who told him that the gold was in that monument. I continued, "Well, once I took the time to think about it I realized that the gold couldn't be inside that rock. One, the rock is solid, and two, the man who had the gold was there at that place 100 years before the monument.

"I'm omitting a lot here, but I came to Texas to visit Jack. I didn't mean to visit him this way. I started out and my car broke down, Bill Knox came to pick me and my car up, and it turned out that he was the one who had delivered the monument here. He brought me up here to see it and Jasper Brown, whom I had met in Kansas, followed me here."

"Did he threaten you?" the sheriff asked me.

"Yeah, he threatened me in Kansas, and he threatened to kill me here."

"Did he threaten you?" the sheriff asked Bill.

"He said he would shoot me if I didn't go get in the truck. Then when I stepped out of the truck and yelled at him, he fired two shots at me."

It took another 30 minutes to get everything checked out. The young cousin that Jasper Brown had forced to come with him was released and allowed to leave. Both Bill and I asked him if he had enough money to get back home, and he said he did. Bill Knox's gun permit was in order and there were no charges placed against him. He had spent most of the time talking to Anita when he wasn't being questioned. Jack Winston came over and wanted to know if I was coming home with him.

"No, this sort of put a bad pall on the day. I'm going to ride back to my hotel with Bill, and from there go home."

"I was looking forward to catching up," Jack said. "Then again, you might be back in Sweetwater sooner than you think. If Brown doesn't plead guilty, I'm sure the D.A. will subpoena you to testify. Judging from reports that the deputies have been giving me tonight from the background searches we have put on him, he's lucky he's not already in jail. Looks like he's just been getting by. Guess his luck just ran out."

"Well, the sun doesn't shine up the same dog's butt every day," I said.

When all the law enforcement personnel had left the area, Anita Walsh asked if we still wanted a glass of lemonade.

"You got time to drink a glass of lemonade?" Bill asked.

"I'm with you," I replied. "I'm free until 9 in the morning, when I have to catch a plane."

I could tell he liked that answer. He didn't seem to be in any hurry to leave the company of Anita Walsh.

While Bill talked to Anita, I sent the pictures to my wife that I had taken with my cell phone. I then called her and told her to e-mail them to the newspapers and television news stations. I didn't tell her anything about what had happened with Jasper Brown.

"I'm not going to tell you where the monument is located, that way you don't have to lie. You can truthfully say you don't know. I will be home tomorrow afternoon and explain why I want it done this way."

Inside Anita's Collectibles, Anita Walsh had quite a collection of everything. I was really impressed by her assortment of first edition books. Being a somewhat semi-half-hearted book collector, I always take time to browse a good collection. She had some winners. I didn't see a biography of Admiral Farragut, but I found a collection of John Hancock's letters in a nice dust cover. I could use it to brush up for my next Stoney Point DAR meeting. The book that really caught my eye was a pristine copy of *Booked to Die* by John Dunning, a first edition, first printing, signed by him. I owned a good copy, but this one looked like it was printed yesterday. Her price was $1,450 dollars. She saw me looking at it and came over to where I was standing.

"I can let you have that copy today for $900," she said.

"I'd love to own this book," I said, "And this is a fair price. I'm going to have to pass today, but if it doesn't sell, I'll be back and get it before long."

I didn't want to tell her that as much as I had spent on airfare, rental cars, motels, and meals on this wild goose chase, the last thing I needed was to go home to my wife with a $900 book. I mean, I've always been crazy, but I'm not insane.

Bill Knox and I had dinner together that evening and breakfast together the next morning. In one day he had saved me from sunstroke and shot the man who was threatening to kill me, and we had become good friends.

"You be sure and let me know if you learn where the gold is, because I want to help dig for it," he said.

"You have my promise that I will call, if and when I know something. You sure you're going to have time to do this? I would think you're going to be spending a lot of time with Ms. Walsh," I kidded.

"I'm going to spend as much time with her as I can," he said.

CHAPTER SIX

A perfect shit storm. That would be the only way to describe the conditions when I arrived at the Knoxville airport.

My wife, Becky, met me there and handed me a copy of the local paper. The pictures of the monument were on the front page, but it was the other article that had things all shook up. The headline read:

MAN TELLS TEXAS MAGISTRATE THERE'S GOLD AT LOWE'S FERRY.

The article said that Jasper Brown from Kansas had appeared before a judge in Abilene, Texas, to prove just cause that he should not stand trial for attempted murder. He had said that there was gold at Lowe's Ferry and there was gold in the Admiral Farragut monument. He had said that a man by the name of Charlie Grant from Knoxville knew about this and had tried to steal the gold from him and his family. Brown said that he had met Grant in Kansas, when Grant was there asking about the monument. Brown had admitted to the judge that he had held a gun on Grant, and had fired the gun at a man named Bill Knox who was with Grant. He claimed that both of them were trying to steal gold that belonged to his family. The judge had postponed the hearing until the next day to find some clarity.

"Everybody in this county is looking for you," my wife said. "Not the police yet, but my guess is they will be next. The phone never stopped ringing. All the local news shows want to interview you, and both local papers. This is crazy. What did you do out there?"

"I ran into a crazy person with more drugs than the local pharmacy," I said.

I had to get this shut up in a hurry; it was messing up my plan. On the ride home, I asked Becky to call the newspapers and tell them I'd give them a quote later today and to call the local newscast and tell them I was ready to talk.

I had three of my own phone calls to make. One to Jack Winston, another to Bill Knox, and the last one to Darwin Brown III. I told all three what I had in mind, and what I needed them to do. As Barney Fife would say, "We got to nip this in the bud."

Darwin Brown made a call to the authorities in Abilene telling them that Jasper Brown had beaten him severely enough to land him in the hospital. He also told them that Jasper was fixated on the subject of gold, and that Jasper had a serious drug problem. Darwin then called my hometown newspapers and television news channels with the same story. Bill Knox made the same calls to the same people. He gave them the facts about how Jasper shot at him and how he returned fire and hit Jasper. He stressed the point that Jasper appeared to be on drugs and was extremely agitated because there was no sign of gold.

Jack Winston went one step farther. After telling his story to the news outlets, he called the local police and told them. All of their efforts seemed to have fallen on deaf ears. I talked to reporters from the newspapers and television, and they were only interested in one thing: Was there really gold at Lowes's Ferry? I had called in a contingent to help, and talked myself blind, trying to convince everyone that Jasper Brown was a couple of sandwiches short of a picnic, only to find out that everyone had gold rush fever.

Nearly two weeks elapsed before the media's fever began to subside and they moved onto more interesting things. There were still sporadic reports, however, of people showing up at Lowe's Ferry to look for the gold. The police arrested a couple of them, and the land owner filed several complaints.

In the meantime, I tried to lie low, while at the same time stressing to anyone who asked me that *there was no gold*. I talked to two of the Daughters of American Revolution chapters about the monument in the vaguest terms. The Stoney Point chapter of the DAR invited me back to speak at their next meeting but I declined. I told the entertainment regent, Mrs. Knight, to book me later when I had more relevant information.

I did ask her what they were serving for lunch. I couldn't resist. She informed me proudly that they were having asparagus casserole and unleavened biscuits sprinkled with dill. For once I didn't have a comeback.

I spent the better part of those two weeks looking everywhere I could for the four remaining letters to my granddad from Sonny Brown. I had lots of questions that I didn't think could be answered until I found them. My aunt had said there had been five letters but my granddad burned them. Why? He kept one; did he keep the rest? And if the letters did mention that there was gold on the place, why didn't he try and find it? The other weird thing was that

Darwin (Sonny) Brown said he was coming back to help my granddad find the gold, but he never showed up again.

I was going through the family pictures again, for what now seemed to be the hundredth time, when I noticed that the seam on one picture album looked uneven to me. On closer examination it looked as if had been slit open and glued back together. I took out my trusty Swiss Army knife that my aunt had given me and stuck it in the tiny seam of the picture album. On the front side of the album beneath the cover were three pieces of paper folded into a square. On the back side of the album were several sheets of paper folded into one square. The papers had turned brown in places because of age, but they were still very much legible. My heart was pounding with anticipation. I was sure this was what I was looking for, and I hurriedly open one of the folded pieces of paper. It was signed Sonny.

I had just found the letters.

For several minutes I just held the letters, looking at them. It amazed me that I had found them at all. These letters were written more than 50 years ago, and I put them into the order that they came before I starting reading them. Letter two, after the first one I had found, was dated July 23, 1956. It was short; Sonny said that the gold was not in the monument. He had misunderstood what his informant had told him. That was a piece of information I could have used before I tore out across the country looking for it. The letter did not mention the gold again. Sonny said that the county still had not set bail, so he would be in jail while longer. He said, "I think I could stand this better if the food was any good. It's awful.

When I do get out I never want to see another undercooked bean and a soggy-assed biscuit." Sounded like a recipe I need to give the Stoney Point chapter of the Daughters of the America Revolution.

Letters three and four were also just one page. Letter three, dated August 16, 1956, basically said "I'm still here and they have not set bail." The letter written September 21, 1956, letter four, said the person who was giving him the information about the gold was a man named Rafael Santo.

Santo had ties to the Mesquida family of Spain—Jorge Farragut's people—and he claimed to have a letter that gave several sites where gold was buried. It was Sonny Brown's belief that the gold had been buried by Jorge Farragut or persons closely associated with him. The letter ended with a post script from Sonny to Granddad: "My wife was here today. She's says that she believes that my sentence is up the middle of next month. I hope she is right."

For the life of me, I couldn't believe that he would not have put that first in the letter. It is strange what the mention of gold does to a man. My hands were shaking as I unfolded and smoothed the pages of letter number five. It was dated May 23, 1957.

Dear Matthew,

I am worried because I have not heard from you. This will be my fifth letter and you have not answered me yet. I hope that you and yours are doing all right.

I am finally out of jail. They released me about two days before Thanksgiving last year. It was a long hard time and I wouldn't want to go through that again. I lost about everything. I did manage to save my farm, but there is nothing there but the house. My wife sold off everything, then left with the rancher that lived about a mile down the road. The funny thing is that she came to see me about every two weeks and never one time mentioned it. When I got out and got home she had left me a letter. Rafael, the man I met in jail, made a joke out of it. He said that his wife ran off with his best friend, and he sure did miss him. I think that's the way I feel.

Speaking of Rafael, he does know where the gold is. I thought when he was talking about it in jail that he was just blowing smoke, but he has made a believer out of me. We went to his house in Florida when we got out and he dug out these letters and maps that he had hidden.

    I couldn't believe the detail that the letters gave. There were maps and instructions, and they had logged a journal of each trip that they made to hide the stuff. So far it all has been accurate. We have found gold in Pascagoula, Mississippi, New Orleans, and along the coast next to Mobile. To put it mildly, we are rich, rich, rich.

    I paid 37 dollars to bail Rafael out of jail. That's the best money I ever spent. He was in there for pouring sugar into gas tanks of police cars in the town of Rusten. He served more than a year because nobody ever checked on him. When I got released I asked if Rafael could go also, and they said sure, as long as somebody paid the $37 court costs.

Gold or gold coins are hard to do anything with. We've been struggling to work it all out. That's why I am just going to tell you where the gold is at your place and not make any effort to help you find it. It's heavy, and it's hard to hide when you are moving it.

According to the maps and papers that Rafael has, there is gold hidden at your place, one quarter of a mile from where the ferry was located. It is due north from the ferry and near a flat rock that is big enough to have a square dance on. Three men brought it up from New Orleans on a boat and met Farragut or some of his buddies and buried it there.

The journal said that the boat arrived there about nine o'clock one night in 1807, and they started to offload and hide the gold. The trip up river from New Orleans had taken over two months. Once during the trip they had been hung up on a sandbar for over a day. They anchored the boat in the Holston and used small row-boats they called punts to haul the gold ashore.

They had dug a hole next to the flat rock and were about to put a chest of gold in when they were attacked by a scouting or hunting party of what was believed to be Cherokee. One of the men in the boat shot one of the Cherokee in the head and the Cherokee came tumbling off the flat rock down to where they were. They also shot another one, but the party carried him off into the woods. The journal said they stuck the Indian in the hole they had dug and covered him up. They then moved to the other side of the flat rock and dug the hole and buried three chests of gold coins, 50 gold bars, and a sprinkling of silver ingots. I have no idea what a sprinkling of silver is.

The journal said that it took them until six O'clock the next morning to get it all buried. The men said that they were paid very well for delivering the gold and helping hide it. The man that they believed to be Jorge Farragut gave them each a bag of gold coins. That seemed to be the pattern each time these gold runners brought in another treasure and hid it. I suppose by the time this was over they were very wealthy men.

That's what I know about the gold. The map I had showed the Holston River and the Lowe's Ferry at Stony Point. Sometimes in the journal it is spelled Stony Point, and in other places it is spelled Stoney Point.

I hope you find the hidden treasure and it serves you well. I have found enough to leave my family and their family in good shape for a long time to come. I have thought long about the fact that I ended up in jail and made friends with an outlaw named Rafael. It seems it was meant to be.

Tell your wonderful wife that I miss her cooking. I loved that sausage gravy she made. I also would like to have a piece of that rhubarb pie she baked. I lost a lot of weight while I was locked up. When I got out, a friend of mine in town asked me if I made it okay. I told him I lost my ass while I was in there. I meant, of course, all of my belongings. He looked at the seat of my pants and said, "I wondered where it went."

I wish you luck with finding the gold. I hope our paths cross again sometime. I will always appreciate your hospitality. Your friend, Sonny

CHAPTER SEVEN

The gold was buried under or near a flat rock about a quarter of a mile from where the ferry was located. I read that part of the letter again, because I couldn't believe what I was reading. There was only one rock like that near that ferry. My cousins and I played on that rock as kids. My heart was pounding. This whole thing was unbelievable, and I couldn't wait to go find the gold.

As excited as I was, one thing puzzled and concerned me. I simply could not understand why my granddad had not tried to find the gold. Life was hard for him on that farm, and yet he made no effort to find a treasure that would have turned his life around. Something didn't add up.

I made another visit to my aunt. I told I her I had found the other letters, and from what I had read granddad had never answered any of them. I wanted to know if she knew of any reason he would hide the letters and not respond. What she told me shook me.

"I don't think he could read," she said. "He hid it from everyone really well, but we always believed he could not read or write."

So it appeared that rather than admit that he could not read, my granddad had pretended to burn the letters. He was just too proud to let it be known that he could not read what Sonny Brown had written him. Granddad and his family were as poor as Job's turkey, scratching out a living on an overworked farm, and they were allegedly sitting on a gold mine.

As British clergyman Charles Caleb Colton once said, "Of all the marvelous works of God, perhaps the one angels view with the most supreme astonishment is a proud man." Preach on, Brother Colton.

Bill Knox had told me on the phone that he would be on the next flight that was headed my way. We spent the first two days going over topography maps I had found and acquired through the internet. The gold was buried in 1807, when a river ran by the property, but thanks to the Tennessee Valley Authority, there was a lake there now. There was a very good chance that the gold was under water. Jorge Farragut had no idea that the river and its bottom land would someday be a lake. We checked the maps to determine where the exact channel of the river had run, but in order to really understand it we were going to have to spend some time on the water. There were a lot of variables. If the land near the river had been flat as it seemed to be on the maps, they probably would not have buried the gold there, because it was good river-bottom farmland. It would have made sense to pick out a landmark like the huge flat rock to hide the gold.

Even if someone had buried something there, someone could have come back and claimed it, or it could have been found by a different party. We were just going to have to pick a spot and dig. We spent one entire day just trying to decide where to dig. We would float by the flat rock, fishing as we went. If we were fishing, we assumed that looked less conspicuous.

Actually we caught several fish. Bill caught a really nice one just north of the rock. We had finally decided after looking at the maps and the lay of the land again that if there was any gold, this north spot was the likely place where it was buried.

That night we came back and started our first attempt at digging. We were wearing hats with lights rigged to them. The rock itself was down a good three feet from the shore line. If we stayed down, we could train the lights on the spot where we were digging and the lights would not be seen from the land. We would just have to be vigilant of night fishermen, if there were any.

The digging was hard. It was almost impossible to find good footing and dig too. One slip and you would be in the lake. We had been digging side by side for about 10 minutes when I heard Bill gasp. I looked and there was a skeleton hand sticking out of the mud. It was the bones of an arm and a hand, fully intact. I dropped to my knees and, for whatever reason, I thought of the Regent, Miss Hancock, and I tasted cucumbers.

Bill looked back at me.

"You having problems?" he asked.

"Just a flashback," I answered.

"Vietnam?"

"No, The Daughters of The American Revolution," I replied.

Using the five-gallon buckets we had brought to put the gold in, we began to throw water on the site to make it look like it had been washed by waves. After we were satisfied that it did not look like an excavating site, we pulled a big piece of driftwood over next to where the arm and hand were sticking out of the ground.

I did that for a reason. In the morning Bill would come here by himself and make the discovery and notify the authorities. If I were there, someone might think it had something to do with the gold. The only thing Bill had to worry about was if they checked the registration on the boat. It would show it belonged to me. His story was going to be that he was up from Texas to do some fishing and I couldn't go, so he borrowed my boat. He would tell the authorities that he had caught his lure on a piece of driftwood, and when he went to free it he had seen an arm and a hand sticking out of the ground. It was the only angle we had, and only time would tell if it would work.

We had no idea what we had dug into. If it was a grave site it might be a long time before we would get to dig, or we may never get to dig on that site again. We would just have to play it by ear. Tomorrow should be interesting to say the least.

Actually it took about four tomorrows to clear it all up. They had dug in the hole we had started, but only found the one skeleton. The skeleton had been identified as belonging to a Native American, probably of Cherokee descent. They had then brought in some archeologist to look for more bones and artifacts, but they found nothing. It appeared that the young man had died from a musket ball at close range roughly 100 years earlier. The authorities had surmised that the killer had buried him or at least covered him over with dirt.

They thanked Bill Knox for his cooperation, and wished him a good vacation. Not once did anyone ask to see registration for the boat. After he reported it the first day, they let him continue on his way and only contacted him after the investigation was over. We followed what was happening on the news and the internet. What was interesting to me was that they had found a Cherokee that had been shot in the head. This had to be the one that was mentioned in the journals that Rafael Santo had shown to Sonny Brown. If that was the case it meant that the gold was on the other side of the rock. We were packing the boat when my cell phone rang. It was Jack Winston.

"You don't have any idea how to get a hold of Bill Knox, do you?" he asked.

"He's standing right here beside me," I answered.

"I need to talk him," Jack said. "His girlfriend Anita Walsh has been kidnapped."

I handed Bill the phone and moved slightly away so as not to eavesdrop on the conversation. He did very little talking, and in a few minutes he handed me back my phone.

"Anita has been kidnapped," he said.

"I heard," I answered. "What did Jack have to say about it?"

"He said that two men came into her shop this morning wearing ski masks. They blindfolded her and led her out. There was one guy waiting in the car, the driver. There was just one customer there in the parking lot when it happened.

After the kidnappers left, that customer, a woman, called the police. There's been no word from the kidnappers. If they want money, they haven't said how much. I've got to check flight schedules and get out there."

"I'm going with you," I said.

"No, there's really no use. Save the air fare. You may be flying back out there pretty soon when Jasper Brown has his hearing. Jack told me they have two thirds of their law enforcement out looking for her. I should have brought her with me, and I will the next time."

"Don't worry about the gold." I said. "If it really is beside that rock, it's been there over 200 years. I doubt it's going anywhere."

There was an available flight at 4:30 that afternoon and Bill Knox was on it. He promised to keep me updated, and would let me know if he needed my assistance. I knew that he cared for Anita Walsh, but I guess I didn't know how much. I would not want to be the kidnappers if Bill Knox caught up to them.

At dinner that night I told my wife that I felt responsible for the entire thing. This gold chasing had caused a chain of events that could prove detrimental to one's health. I thought I was going to get killed by Jasper Brown, and Jasper had taken a couple of shots at Bill Knox. And now Anita Walsh had been kidnapped, and although I didn't know for sure if the gold had anything to do with that, I believed it did.

"My finding that letter and wanting to search for that gold has caused a lot trouble," I said. "I really feel bad that I started all this. Just the mention of a treasure makes idiots out of otherwise sane men."

My wife's answer, "I guess there's no fool like a gold fool," didn't make me feel any better.

CHAPTER EIGHT

Anita Walsh was released later the same day she was captured, and back home before Bill's flight arrived. She had been kept in a bedroom of a house. She never saw the faces of her captors. She did know that one of them stood guard and twice brought her bottled water and a candy bar. The bedroom had an adjoining bathroom and there was a chair in one corner. Her blindfold was removed when she was pushed inside the room. Later during the day she heard a vehicle drive up to the house and then she heard it leave. After a few minutes she checked the door and it opened. She came out of the bedroom into the living room, picked up the phone and called 911. The police were there in less than 10 minutes. All this information I received from a Bill Knox phone call.

"She was scared to death," Bill said. "She had no idea where she was. When she came out of the bedroom she was expecting some kind of trick, and she was surprised that no one was there. She couldn't tell the police where she was, but of course they knew from the 911 call."

"Was she okay?" I asked.

"She was fine," Bill replied. "When the police got there they heard someone hollering out back and they found the home owner tied up in a shed. He said that three men had come to the door, and he didn't know that they had ski masks on until he opened it. They forced their way in, tied his hands, and took him out to the shed. Once in the shed they had tied him to a Warm Morning heater. He didn't know Anita was there until the police came. He thought they were robbing his house. They could find nothing out of place. They even brought the water and the candy they gave Anita."

"Do they have any clues?" I asked.

"Nope, they just know it was three men. The eye witness that saw them over at Anita's place was only able to give the police the color of the van. It was a maroon van, and the woman was not sure of the model or make. She said she thought it looked like a Dodge, but she didn't know. Now here's the interesting part. When I got to Anita's the first thing I noticed was there were little chips of rock and rock dust all around the monument. They had tried to beat it open with a sledge hammer. There were also signs that they had tried to break it open with some kind of chisel. Whoever it was sure didn't believe there wasn't anything to see inside that monument."

"Well, we know who's behind that. Old Jasper is running his gold operation from the county jail."

"That's all it could be," said Bill. "There would be no way that anyone else would think there was gold in a marker made of solid marble."

"He's a hardheaded asshole," I said.

"If I ever get the chance I'm going to see how hardheaded he really is," Bill said. "I'm going to place some bumps up there that he's not going to soon forget. Two or three are for having Anita kidnapped, and two or three for shooting at me. Then I'm really going to pour it on him for shooting my truck. I would rather he shot me than my truck."

"Well, be careful and don't break your hand when you are inflicting that kind of pain."

"You don't use your hands to give him the kind of bumps I'm going to give him," Bill said. "That's the reason God made baseball bats."

The summons to appear at the hearing of Jasper Brown was delivered by a deputy while I was still talking to Bill. He read a part to me and I signed for the papers. Next Tuesday I was supposed to be in court in Abilene, Texas, for a hearing to decide if Jasper Brown should stand trial for attempted murder and other charges. I was informed that my flight would be paid for and my lodging needs met for one day. Bill said that he had not received his summons yet, but he was sure it was coming. I told him I would be in touch when I found out what time my flight got there.

Jack Winston called me later that evening, just after Becky and I had finished dinner.

"Did you get your summons?" he asked.

"It was delivered to me today," I answered. "Listen, if you can make it I would like to have dinner with you on Tuesday night. I've got a business deal you might be interested in."

"What does it consist of?" Jack asked.

"I'd rather discuss it in person and not over the phone," I said.

If we found gold, and there was as much of it as we suspected there was, the logistics around it would be staggering. I wondered if we would have to report it under some treasure law. Also, the need to convert the gold to cash posed another problem. Bill and I needed help with this and we needed someone we could trust. Jack Winston might not be able to help, but I knew he could be trusted.

I took my boat and went by where I thought the gold was hidden again before I left for Abilene. Everything looked the same. As ready as I was to get back to digging, I was even more ready to put Jasper Brown away. He was obsessed by the gold. As long as he was in his hometown jail, he had access to his cronies, and he could stir up trouble. Tomorrow would be a step to get him to a trial that would have him locked away among strangers. However, if his lawyer went for an insanity plea they would probably win. After all, crazy is as crazy does. Jasper Brown was not only crazy but mean, too, and that made me want to put him away that much more.

The note I had waiting for me at the hotel said that the hearing had been postponed until 3 o'clock Tuesday. No other explanation. I called Jack Winston and told him that I was at the hotel, and he said he would meet me in the lobby at seven. My next call was to Bill Knox. He said that he would pick me up at the hotel at eight the next morning. He said that Anita wanted to make us breakfast, and then we could leave there and go to the hearing.

"Does the late start time for the hearing cause you any problems with catching your flight back home?" Jack Winston asked me after we were seated at the sports bar and restaurant he had picked out.

"No, I'm not scheduled out until nine the next morning."

"Well, I've racked my brain wondering about this business deal, so what's it about? Jack asked.

"Gold," I said.

"You've got gold?"

"No, but I hope to have some soon," I said

"How much gold do you hope to have?" Jack asked, checking the score on the baseball game playing above our heads.

"I think there might be a great deal of it," I said. "I figure about five million dollars in gold bars, and I don't know how much more is buried with it. I also believe there is some silver with it."

"Where is this gold?" Jack asked.

"I'm not sure. I think I know, and I think I can get to it. What I wanted to ask you if you knew of anyone that could help get it out of the country and converted to cash. I don't want you involved with anything that is illegal, but I am going to need help."

"Well, I'm not going to do anything illegal, and I'm not going to let you do anything illegal if I can help it," Jack said.

"I don't know if there are any rules about having to report it," I said. "I know in Great Britain they have a treasure act but I don't know about in America. When and if I find the gold I want to have a way to turn it into cash. It's going to be a great problem just moving as much gold as I think there is. I may have to move it a little at a time. What I wanted you to do was find the way to do all that. I promise you a very healthy share of the treasure for your work."

The next hour was spent discussing options. Once the baseball game was over and I had his full attention, Jack had a lot of questions. I tried to answer them, but I would not tell where the gold was. Jack was concerned that any action that he took could be breaking the law.

"I came to you because I thought you might know the right people to get this done without causing too much of a stir. I realize that payments will have to be made for people that help. I just need to know if you know the right people."

"I know people from all walks of life," Jack said. "I know people from the lowliest street walker out there on Second Avenue to the governor, and I am convinced I could get it done. I just don't know how much will be legal and how much will be breaking the law."

"You are going to be rich if this works out," I said.

"How many people know about this?" he asked.

"Just me, Bill Knox, and now you," I replied.

"Can Knox be trusted?" Jack asked.

"Of course he can. I can't see any reason not to trust him."

"I'm not knocking him," Jack said. "The kind of money you are talking about causes people to do strange things. You've only known him a couple of weeks or so. I stand a lot to lose here. I just want to be sure of the players."

"You also stand a lot to gain if I find that gold. Tell your boss what I'm going to tell mine."

"What's that?" he asked.

"Kiss my ass, I bought a boat," I answered.

"What's that mean?" he asked.

"It's from a Lyle Lovett song, called 'If I Had a Boat.'"

"I need to get out more or quit bumping in to you," Jack said.

I just nodded my head in agreement.

Although I was going to see Jack tomorrow at the hearing, I told him that I would call him when I found the gold. He said he would stay in touch and let me know if he found any angles on moving and selling the gold. He apologized that he couldn't see me for breakfast in the morning but the District Attorney wanted to see all the officers that were involved the night Jasper Brown threatened me and took shots at Bill Knox. I told him that I had already accepted breakfast at Anita Walsh's.

"I don't know anything about his defense attorney," Jack told me. "If I did I would share it with you."

"I plan to answer everything he asks me truthfully," I said. "I don't need a jail sentence for perjury in Texas."

"The judge who will be at the hearing will put you in the mind of the last commanding officer we had on that destroyer we were on. He looks like his eyebrows have been stitched together to keep that scowl on his face. He is a no-nonsense guy and pretty mean to everybody."

"Nothing like good old Texas justice," I said. "Oh, by the way, tell Linda that Becky and I asked about her, and we'd love to see her sometime."

Jack hesitated. "Linda and I are not together anymore."

"When did that happen?" I asked.

"About six months ago. She said she was tired of being a detective's wife, and she wanted a change. She took a job in Houston and I haven't seen her since. We're still married – she hasn't done anything about getting a divorce – but I've talked to her once on the phone, and that's it."

"I'm really sorry," I said.

"Well, you know, things happen, people change, and time goes on."

"Is there anything I can do to help?" I asked.

"No, I'm fine. If I don't get to see you after the hearing, I'll be in touch. You know, when life hands you lemons, you make chicken salad."

"Yeah, and when it hands you chicken shit, you make lemonade."

We'd always turned those sayings around and laughed about it. Today it didn't seem funny.

CHAPTER NINE

The next morning when I was waiting in the lobby for Bill Knox, Jack walked in.

"I didn't expect to see you here," I said.

"They just called me about a half an hour ago and told me to drop by and pick up the medical expert that the prosecution had flown in, and take him to the briefing we're having this morning."

Bill Knox walked in just as Jack had excused himself to go talk to the desk clerk. We waited until he finished and came back to where we were standing.

"Man, I tell you. We never know what's going on." Jack said. "The desk clerk told me that the guy already left. The desk clerk called a cab for him. I hope we handle the hearing better than we handled setting it up. If we don't, Jasper Brown may be a free man this afternoon."

"You're welcome to join us for breakfast," Bill Knox said to Jack as we all three walked to the parking lot.

"Nothing I would like better, but duty calls. I'll see you guys at the hearing."

Anita Walsh was a really good cook. In addition to that she was very pretty, and very nice. The omelets and Belgian waffles were done to perfection and the homemade syrup was out of this world. Bill Knox was a lucky man. As we ate I asked her about the kidnapping ordeal.

"They just walked in and took me away," she said. "I didn't even notice them at first. When I looked up I saw two guys standing there with ski masks over their face. One of them was holding a gun and he told me to stick out my hands. When I did he put a pair of handcuffs on my wrist. They then told me to come with them. I was trying to stall in hopes a customer would drive up, so I asked if I could lock up the place. The one holding the gun told me I could. I asked if I could get my keys and he said yes to that. It was a very low-keyed event."

"So they were calm?" I asked.

"They were very calm. They acted like this happened every day. After I locked the door and managed to push the keys in my jean pockets, the one not holding the gun said, 'I'm going to blindfold you.' He took out a white scarf and tied it around my head and over my eyes. We walked down the walk with one of them leading me. When we got to the car, the one without the gun told the other one to get in the back, and he would put me in the back on the other side. Then he got into the front and we drove away. It wasn't until they started talking that I realized there was third person."

"Did they talk about where they were going to take you?" I asked.

"They didn't even know where they were going to take me. They didn't have a clue. The two in the front seat were arguing with the one in the back seat. Finally the one in the back seat told the driver to find a house with an outside building – that he had a plan. So they drove around on different roads until he spotted what they wanted, I guess. The one in the back seat told the other two to guard me and he got out of the car. I guess that's when he took the old man out to the building and tied him up, and then he came back and got me. The other two talked about him the whole time he was gone. They were tired of him yelling at them and bossing them around. To be honest, the two in the front seat didn't seem very bright."

"Well, you need to find someone to run your business and come back with Bill. I talked to Becky last night and she told me to make sure you knew you were welcome to stay with us."

"I'm taking my RV," said Bill. "If you don't care, I can park it on your property. I can also use it to transport the gold if we find any."

"My nephew is going to keep the shop open for me," said Anita. "He's trying to decide if he wants to go back to college or not. I'd say some time spent greeting the public will get him back to school real fast."

We finished the conversation with more coffee and once again I looked through Anita's book collection. I took out three $100 bills and handed them to Anita.

"This is a down payment on the book I want," I told her. "Hold it for me until we get this mess settled. Maybe if they lock Jasper Brown in jail his idiot buddies will calm down."

Bill and I both declined Anita's offer to make us sandwiches for lunch. The breakfast we had put away would sustain us for awhile. We said our goodbyes and left. About a mile down the two-lane road that led from Anita's to the main highway, we met a maroon van. About 200 feet from us the driver of the van pulled into our lane and came at us, almost meeting us head-on. With very little time left to avoid a collision, Bill left the road. We were tearing down small bushes and bouncing over rough uneven ground. Bill held on and in one smooth motion put his truck back onto the road. We sat there shaking.

"Holy shit, what was that all about?" Bill asked.

"That's that maroon van that the customer saw at Anita's when they kidnapped her. They know it's us. They're trying to keep us from going to the hearing."

"Hearing or no hearing, I'm going back to check on Anita. I can't believe I was stupid enough to leave her there by herself."

With the U-turn completed, we started back to Anita's shop. We probably had gone a tenth of a mile when we saw the van coming back at us. Bill stopped his truck and reached for his pistol.

"Get out," he said.

I got out of the truck, still standing by the passenger's side, and Bill stepped around in front. The van was coming at a high rate of speed, headed straight toward him. At about 25 feet Bill opened fire. The first shot took out the windshield. I don't know where the other shots went. I do know they hit the van, and that the van went off the side of the road and hit a large rock and went rolling over. It was like watching an action movie with the scenes out of order.

We stood and watched as three men climbed out of the van. One was holding his arm in an abnormal manner and I assumed it was broken. The men were too far away to make out any facial features. Without speaking we got back into the truck and went back for Anita. She put up a good argument for staying, but Bill would not be swayed. She locked up the shop and we headed for the hearing.

There was no way we were going to make it on time. The maroon van was still on its side as we sped by. Farther down the road we saw the three men walking. As we approached they stuck their thumbs into the air in order to hitch a ride. My first thought was I sure am glad one of them or all of them did not pull a pistol and start firing. Bill's answer was to speed up and get as close to the edge of the payment as he could. Our last image of the men was their headlong dives off the payment into the rattlesnake-infested brambles. If I were judging the dives in a competition, I would have given them each a four on style.

Jack Winston answered his cell phone after several rings.

"We are going to be late to the hearing," I told him. "We just got ran off the road by three guys in a maroon van. I'm guessing it's the same three men who kidnapped Anita Walsh."

"When and where?" Jack asked.

"Just a little while ago, not far from Anita Walsh's place. They wrecked their van and they are walking toward the main road. The van is lying on its side about 10 yards off the road."

"I'll get a patrol car out there," Jack said. "I'll also try to soften the blow here with the judge, but he is not going to be too happy."

While I had Jack on the phone, I asked him why Anita had not been asked to testify at today's hearing. In fact she had never been questioned. He said that as far as he could tell, the prosecution had decided that mine and Bill's testimony was enough to persuade the judge to send Jasper Brown's case to a grand jury. I also asked if the young man that Jasper Brown had forced to drive him from Kansas was going to testify.

"He was in a serious car accident," Jack answered. "Someone ran him off the road. He's in the hospital."

"I suppose no one checked it out to see if it was related to any of this," I said.

"I don't have any jurisdiction in Kansas," was Jack's answer.

It's the age of instant communication. You can know what kind of cereal someone is having for breakfast before they have time to pour the milk over it, but you can't contact a another police department in Kansas? I decided not to make that comment to Jack. I had been to Texas twice and felt my life was in danger both times. I needed all the allies I could get.

CHAPTER TEN

Taylor County courthouse in Abilene, Texas, is architectural structure at its finest. A work of art, one whose details take time to appreciate. Unfortunately we didn't have the time. Bill, Anita and I jumped out of the truck and ran for the courthouse door. The bailiff met us at the door and ushered us straight into the judge's chamber. Sitting in a huge overstuffed back chair, behind a solid oak desk that was polished until the shine hurt your eyes, was the sternest face I had ever seen on a human being. Remember when your mother used to say stop making those faces, because your face will freeze that way? It was too late. His had frozen.

"You are three quarters of an hour late. You have made a mockery of this court, you have inconvenienced people, you have held up important matters of the law, just because you did not see fit to be on time. I have no patience with people who disrespect my court. If the hearing is set at three, I fully expect you to be here at three. But because of your selfishness, and your total disregard for this procedure, you show up three-quarters of an hour late. I want to know why."

I tried to explain. "We were on our way here and we were run off the road by three men in a maroon van. We got back onto the road and they came back and tried to run us off again," I said. I went on to tell him that it looked like the description we had of the same van and the same three men who had kidnapped Anita at gunpoint. "We went back to Ms. Walsh's place of business to get her to come with us because we feared for her safety. I called the lead detective on the case and told him to let you and everyone know we would be late. It was never our intent to disrupt, or disrespect this court. These three men kidnapped her and now have tried to do harm to Bill and me. My guess is that it is to keep us from testifying at this hearing. I think they are doing this for Jasper Brown."

The judge never even acted like I had said anything about the three men. They could have held up a bank and took us as hostages, but it would not have mattered. He was so hung up on the fact we were late, he was not hearing anything else.

"Ms. Walsh, I am sorry about your ordeal," the judge said to Anita. "I am sure the authorities are conducting a proper investigation." He turned his attention to me and Bill. "However, I don't find this to be an acceptable excuse. The lead detective is not the person that you need to report to. You should have called the court clerk. That said, it would have not made a difference to me. You should have left earlier. You should have expected the unexpected. I admire the fact that you went back because you thought Ms. Walsh could be in danger, but I can't and won't accept this. If you are scheduled for a hearing or a trial in this court and you die the night before, I expect them to roll your casket through here before the proceedings start."

He stood up. "Now, we need to get out there and get this thing underway. There will be a fine for you gentlemen to pay. You will need to see Mrs. Crawford out front before you go to make a charitable contribution to our county's no-kill pet shelter. She will tell you what the fine is when you see her. But to give you a hint, you might want to pull a Ben Franklin photo out of your pocket before you get there. Ms.

Walsh, you are also welcome to make a donation on your own. By the way, gentlemen, it is tax deductable."

Following behind the bailiff, we went back into the court room and took our seats. Jasper Brown was already there, sitting at the left front of the room. About a minute later the bailiff instructed everyone to rise, and the judge came in. As soon as everyone was seated, he wasted no time getting started. Banging his gavel and calling the court to order, he explained that the reason for the hearing was to determine if Jasper Brown should face charges for assault with a deadly weapon and attempted murder. He then asked the prosecution for their opening statement.

The prosecutor opened by telling the court that Jasper Brown was a dangerous person. He had threatened me, tried to shoot Bill Knox, and had beaten his father so badly that his father was still in the hospital. The prosecutor said that all of this could be proven and that it should be enough to keep Jasper Brown off the street and locked away from society. The prosecutor told the judge that the prosecution's part would be brief. He only planned to call two people to testify, me and Bill Knox, and he would play a tape from Darwin Brown III.

Mark Nixon was the defense attorney's name. He was very young, and was introduced as Jasper Brown's court-appointed attorney. Nixon's face spoke volumes about the fact that he would rather be anywhere in the world than in that Abilene courtroom defending Jasper Brown. He was one unhappy camper. He spoke in very low tones, and the judge asked him not once but twice to speak up. Nixon said that his client had acted harshly when he believed that something that was rightfully his was being stolen from him. He said he now believed his client was sorry, now realized his mistakes, and wanted a new chance. Nixon wanted to end it today with time served, and set Jasper Brown free. Nixon asked the court for liberty to question me and Bill Knox. He didn't say that he would put Brown on the stand. Brown was wearing an orange jump suit. His feet were shackled and his hands were cuffed. He never did look at his attorney. It was if the two had never met.

I swore to tell the truth and nothing but the truth and was asked to be seated.

"When was the first time you ever met Jasper Brown?" The prosecutor asked me.

"On his father's front porch outside Hutchinson, Kansas," I answered.

"Did he threaten you then?" he asked.

"He said that he would take legal action against me, or come hunt me down."

"What was his reason for this?"

"Somehow he thinks that I stole some gold from him," I said.

"Did you?" he asked.

"No, I never did find any gold," I answered.

Jasper Brown jumped up from his seat, handcuffs, shackles, and all.

"He's a liar. He's lying through his teeth," Brown said. "He stole that gold. He knew where it was. Why don't you people do something about that?"

The judge was beating the desk with the gavel, and Brown's attorney was trying to get Brown to sit down. Only after the judge sent an officer over to where Brown was did he sit down and quit yelling.

"If that happens again, Mr. Brown," the judge said, "You will be removed from this room and we will continue without you. You will also be fined at the court's discretion. I will not tolerate any more outbursts."

I finished answering the prosecutor's questions. He asked me why I came to Kansas, why I came to Texas and if I had talked to Darwin Brown III. I told him that Darwin had called me from the hospital and told me that Jasper had beaten him in order to find out where I was going. He asked if at one time I believed that there was gold in the Farragut marker. I was also asked about the letter that Darwin Brown's grandfather sent to my grandfather.

One question was all the defense attorney asked me.

"Why did you not believe there was gold in the marker?"

"Two main reasons," I answered. "One its solid rock, there's no way to put the gold in there. Number two reason, the person who was supposed to have put the gold in the marker lived there from around 1794 until 1808. The marker didn't exist until 1900."

Bill Knox took his turn next and answered questions about the shooting incident.

"Did you shoot at Jasper Brown?" the prosecutor asked Bill.

"I returned fire after he fired at me twice and missed."

The next few minutes were spent with Bill answering questions about shooting Jasper. He also answered questions about why he had a gun in his truck and whether it was legal.

On cross-examination, the defense asked Bill if he was shooting to kill.

"I was not shooting to kill him," Bill replied.

"But there was a possibility that you could have killed him, right?" asked the defense attorney.

"I have three proclamations that state I am an expert with a handgun," said Bill. "I hit exactly where I was aiming. At that range if I had meant to kill him, then I would have."

In the final summation the prosecution played the tape that Darwin Brown III had sent. The tape said that Jasper had always been a problem child. He had stolen since he was a small boy. He had beaten his mother and now he had beaten his father, too. He would not go to school, and he formed gangs that did what he said or he hurt them, too. Jasper had told his dad that he was going to find me in Texas, and if I didn't share the gold he was going to make me pay. The tape was a saga of a child gone wrong.

Proverbs 19:17 says "Chasten thy son while there is hope, and let not thy soul spare for his crying." It appeared that Darwin Brown III did not chasten, abandoned hope, and gave into the crying.

The judge made his ruling immediately after the defense rested. He said that Jasper Brown would have to stand trial for attempted murder. Addressing the issues, he said that he found mine and Bill Knox's testimony to be credible. He said that the tape that he had allowed to be played had no bearing on his decision.

"What I have heard here this afternoon and the behavior of Jasper Brown leads me to believe that he is a danger to society," the judge said. "So bail is denied without debate. A trial will be set, the time to be announced. Mr. Grant and Mr. Knox, I remind you to stop by and see Mrs. Crawford before you leave the building. Failure to do so will be viewed as contempt. Mr. Nixon I ask you to join me in my chambers. Officers, please return the prisoner to his proper housing. This hearing is dismissed."

"Wonder why he wants to see the defense lawyer?" I asked.

"It's probably about the fact that he didn't represent his client very well," Jack said. "That was pathetic. He did nothing to defend him. The question he asked you about the gold favored the prosecution more than the defense. He should have portrayed Brown as being insane, because I think he really is. Maybe that's why he didn't get another lawyer; maybe he is crazy."

"Crazy mean," I said. "Did you see the look he was giving me when he was saying I was lying about the gold? If he had had a gun he would have shot me there."

"Yeah, that little outburst didn't help his cause any," said Jack. "I swear I believe that attorney was bought off by the prosecution. I don't think in all the cases and trials I have been involved with have I ever seen anyone represented so poorly. Jasper Brown, if he had a brain at all should ask for another lawyer, and another hearing.

I wondered for a second whose side Jack was on, exactly, but what I said was, "Well, I've had all of Texas justice I can stand for the time being," I said. "Does anyone want to get something to eat?"

"Don't forget, we have to go shell out some money before we can leave," Bill said.

"Let's go meet Mrs. Crawford," I said.

CHAPTER ELEVEN

After we paid our fines, Bill and Anita declined the invitation to go eat with me and Jack, heading back to her place instead. Bill knew I was going to fly back home that night, and he said that he would have everything in order here and that he and Anita would see me in 10 days or less.

Jack drove us to a sub shop about a mile from the court house. Over a Cajun sub and a bag of jalapeno chips, he told me that he had found some persons who might convert the gold to cash.

"I know you get tired of me asking this," he said, "but how many people actually know about this treasure you're hunting?"

"Five," I answered. "Six if you count Darwin Brown III out in Kansas. However, he has assured me that he wants none of the gold and has no intentions of coming to look for it. So that leaves me, you, Becky, Bill Knox and Anita Walsh."

"And you are sure that Bill Knox can be trusted?"

"Yes. The man can be trusted," I said. "He's as honest as the day is long. Why do you keep asking me if he's honest?"

"Because getting the gold changed over to cash is something that not everyone needs to know about," Jack said. "I'm checking the legality of it. It could be a federal crime. Believe me, I'm not about to throw a lifelong career away and go to prison, too. Cops don't need to be in prison. They don't last very long in there."

"So, can you trust the people you've got lined up to make the exchange?" I asked.

"As much as you can trust someone like that," he said. "You know they're crooks or they wouldn't be in that kind of business. Actually, they live closer to you than me. They have a cabin outside of Gatlinburg. I am supposed to meet with them in about two weeks. I will know then what the deal is and if we need to go that route. If it looks shady I will just cancel it. All they know now is that there could be a large amount of gold. I will check with you on my way up there and find out if you have found any. You really do believe there is gold on that place?"

"Yeah, I really do," I replied. I told him about digging up the skeleton of the Cherokee brave and how it had made a believer out of me. "He had been shot in the head, just as Sonny Brown wrote about to my granddad." I explained that we would have kept digging except for the delay about the skeleton. "Then we had to come here for the trial."

"How are you going to move the gold when you find it?" Jack asked.

"We don't have all the details worked out, but we will when Bill gets to Tennessee," I said.

We finished our meal with small talk and he gave me a ride to the airport. I asked about Linda and he told me that she had gotten tired of him being on so many demanding cases, working such long hours and not taking any time off. Before she got her own lucrative job in Houston, she begged him to try and find another job.

"You know me," he said. "I've always have been a workaholic."

"All work and no play can make Jack a dull boy," I replied.

"I'd like to have a nickel for every time I've heard that bullshit," Jack said.

It reminded me that my own first order of business when I got home was to work on my retirement. I had often talked about retiring but had never gone that extra mile to get it done. It took almost three days of talking on the phone and faxing papers, but I finally got it worked out. I had a little more than three weeks' vacation left, and when it was over, I was retired.

I was glad. If it hadn't been for the idea that there was gold out there I would have probably stayed on, but I was happy with the amount I was going to receive, and if I never found an ounce of gold I could still make it. The company had changed dramatically in the years I had been there, and the new style of management had managed the place into the ground. They thought more about how to better their careers than what was best for the company. Old dinosaurs like me needed to move on.

I declined the idea of a retirement party and got busy working on plans of how to move the gold. The gold had been there for over 200 years, but I had this fear it was going to be discovered before we could dig it out. I kept wishing Bill Knox would hurry and get here.

It was on Thursday of the same week that I got a frightening surprise. Around sunrise, my wife came back inside with the two morning papers and said that there was something in the mailbox.

"Why didn't you get it out?" I asked.

"It's not mail or papers," she said. "It's alive. When you get close it makes a pecking noise. It sounds like something hitting on the inside of the mail box."

"So you didn't open it up to see what it was?" I asked.

The look she gave me told me how stupid that question was.

"Okay," I said. "When it gets lighter, I will go down there and take a look."

"It's just making this clicking like sound," she said. "I got the paper out of the tube attached to the mailbox and the thing just went crazy making that noise."

I finished my coffee and decided that it was time to go take a look. I went to the back deck and got the long grill tongs. The longer I had sat there drinking coffee, the more my brain had conjured up images of rabid squirrels or raccoons, although I wasn't sure how either would have gotten in and closed the lid. I could see something chomping down on my hand. As I approached the box, I heard the clicking sound. My wife was right; whatever was in the mailbox was alive.

I reached out with the tongs and pulled the lid of the mailbox open. What popped its head out froze me in my tracks. I quickly slammed the mailbox door shut with the tongs. My hands were shaking so bad I couldn't control them. What had stuck its head out of my mailbox was a snake. Not just any kind of snake. I recognized the shape of the head and the distinct markings. The reptile making the clicking sound inside my mailbox was a diamondback rattlesnake.

The next thought that hit me stunned me as much as finding the snake had: We don't have rattlesnakes where I live. We do in the mountains nearby, but not here. The snake didn't crawl in there, and it sure didn't shut the lid behind itself. It was placed in there. Somebody was trying to kill me.

My next thought was of Jasper Brown and how bad I wished that Bill Knox wasn't a shooting expert. A shot between the eyes would have served us all well.

I went back into the house, and poured another cup of coffee.

"Did you find out what it was?" my wife asked.

"It was a huge diamondback rattlesnake," I answered.

"Of course it was," she said. "That's why I didn't get it out when I was down there."

"It's a good thing you didn't. It's a big one and enough poison to stop a locomotive."

"You're serious," she said.

"Very serious," I answered. "It couldn't have gotten in there by itself. Somebody put it there."

"Why?"

"I think somebody is trying to kill me," I said.

After some thought I went to my tool shed and picked up a glass aquarium with a lid that had been there for about two years. It had once been the home of my granddaughter's iguana. The iguana had lived a good life but had given up the ghost one morning for reasons unknown to us, and it was now buried in the back yard. I had been meaning to get rid of the aquarium, but for some reason had kept it around. It had a lid with air holes that fit snuggly.

I had no idea why I had decided to keep the snake, but something was telling me that's what I needed to do. A long-handled hoe was hanging from a peg on the wall of the shed and I grabbed that also. While my intentions were to catch the snake alive, I had no qualms about chopping off its head if push came to shove. I came back through the house and asked my wife to get my digital camera and follow me to the mailbox. I wanted a picture of me capturing the snake.

I once again, this time very cautiously, opened the lid on the mailbox. The snake was not visible at first, and did not stick his head out. I waited for a little while, and then I saw the snake take a peek outside. His tongue was flicking back and forth, and chills were running down my spine. I reached for his head with the tongs and got him tight the first try. He was wiggling like a fish on a hook and he was hard to hold. He was throwing his body, trying to hook my arm. I could feel perspiration forming on my brow, and knew it was not because of the morning sun. My wife was frantically snapping pictures as I dropped him into the aquarium and pushed the lid shut with the toe of my shoe.

Mission accomplished. I was admiring my handy-work when my wife screamed and pointed toward the mailbox. Coming out of the box and lowering itself to the ground was a rattler bigger than the first one. There had been two snakes in the mailbox. I have never wet my pants, but I can say now that I once came mighty close.

Rattlesnake number two had no intentions of hanging around. It was moving away as fast as it could slither. I picked up the hoe and the tongs and went running after him. The snake made it to a smoke bush tree and decided to make his stand at its base. I got there at the same time and pulled it away from the tree with the hoe. The snake opened its mouth and showed those long fangs. My wife flipped the dial on the camera to the camcorder and recorded my capture of the snake.

I will admit it does not show me in a very brave light. Every time the snake would try to coil, I would drag it back out from the base of the tree with the hoe. It was my belief that the snake had to be coiled before it could strike at you, but it could still make some long lunges when it was not coiled. Each time it did that I would retreat, and have to find my courage and go after the snake again. It was a lengthy battle, with the snake getting nastier after each encounter. With the help of the long-handled hoe and the large grilling tongs, I managed to get it into the aquarium with the other one. It was not a pretty sight and it took longer than it should have, but the snake was captured and I did not get bitten.

I took the snakes in their glass container and placed them on a shelf in the outside shed. I was amazed how heavy the snakes were. I had no idea what I would have to feed them, and I didn't know how I could give them water. I still had no idea what I was going to do with them, but I had a gut feeling I needed to keep them alive. To try to calm down some, I retrieved some information off the internet on how to take care of them, and I looked up Tennessee gun laws.

It wasn't until the next day that my wife found the handwritten note in the mailbox. It said that the snakes were a gift from some of my friends in Texas. I can't imagine what they would have given me if they had been my enemies.

CHAPTER TWELVE

By the time that Bill and Anita had arrived the following Wednesday I had taken a half-day state-approved shooting course and was waiting to find out if I had passed the test required for a handgun permit. I had never seen the need to have a gun-carry permit before, but recent happenings had changed my mind. It was becoming quite obvious that someone meant to do me harm. What started out to be a fun jaunt looking for a lost monument had turned into deadly game, and it appeared I was one of the players, whether or not I wanted to be.

It took no time at all to get Bill Knox's RV hooked up to some electricity and water, and even a shorter time for my wife and Anita Walsh to become friends. That night, after a fine dinner, Bill and I went over our plans on how we were going to acquire the gold. I honestly believed there was gold there, and I knew we had looked at it from all angles. One of the things that had been bothering me was how we were going to disguise where we were digging. We planned to dig at night, but in the day it would be quite easy to see that there had been activity at that spot and someone was going to stop and investigate. That was one thing we didn't need. My idea was to cut honeysuckle and other vines and weave them together and place them over the freshly dug space when we finished each night. I realized that we would have to change the vines out when they died, but it was the only idea I had. Only after we had hung them over the digging site would we know if it actually worked.

So that next morning Bill and I loaded up in my extended cab truck and headed to the woods. After a whole day spent collecting the vines, threading them together, and placing them in a barrel full of water to slow down the wilting process, I was beginning to wonder if this was such a great idea. Feeling sorry for us, my wife and Anita had agreed to cut some more vines and string them together if we needed them. Although Bill and I were both eager to get started, we needed to check the site out from the boat once more during daylight, and as the four of us ate another fine dinner, we made plans to do that the next morning. Then, when it got dark, we'd start to dig.

It seemed to me like it had been months instead of weeks, but at last we were going to put our plan to work. What I didn't yet know was that there were others waiting for us to put our plan into action, too. We were about to meet them.

Bill and I were out on the lake early. We had stopped to eat at a breakfast restaurant that I liked and still had made it to the water before 8 o'clock. There had been just enough morning clouds to ensure a beautiful sunrise, but they had dissipated, and the day had all the indications that it was going to be a hot one. We moved up the shore line, casting like we always did when we were trying to be inconspicuous. By the time we had moved in front of where we intended to dig later that night, Bill had caught two nice bass. We had moved slightly past the site when we noticed a boat headed down the lake toward us. My radar went off at once. There were three persons in the boat. If there had been one, or two,

I probably would have never thought anything about it, but three put me on alert.

"Get ready for anything," I said. "My money says that that is the same three guys that tried to run us off the road, and probably the same three that put the rattlesnakes in my mailbox."

The boat slowed as it got closer, and when they were really near, the driver of the boat cut the engine and they drifted up beside us.

"Do you guys know where Lowe's Ferry is?" the driver asked.

"You passed it if you were coming down the lake," I answered. "It's up there around that big bend in the lake," I lied.

"We didn't come down the lake," the driver said. "We've only been up the lake as far as that big house that sits on the hill over on the left side."

"What are you looking for at Lowe's Ferry?" I asked.

"We're looking for where Admiral Farragut was born," the guy said.

"Well, follow me up the lake here," I told them. "I'll take you up there."

The three men were in an aluminum john boat with a 55 h.p. Johnson on the back. I was in a bass boat with more than four times the horse power, so I throttled way back so they could keep up. I took them up the lake to another place where the road dead-ended into the lake. From my research, I knew there had been a ferry in operation there at the same time there was one in operation at Lowe's Ferry. I pulled the boat in close to the old road and waited for them to catch up.

"Here you are," I said. "This is Lowe's Ferry."

"Where was Admiral Farragut born?" the man that had done all the talking asked.

"On that property right there where that house is standing," I said, pointing up the hill from the lake.

"Where was his monument?" the man asked.

"It was right there on the corner of that lot," I lied again. "It's gone now, though. They say it went to Texas."

"Did they call this place Stoney Point?" the man asked.

"There used to be a sign over on the other side that said Stoney Point," I said. "It had an arrow on it that pointed this way. I don't know if it's still over there or not."

The man was real polite; he thanked me for helping them, and we started our boat and sped off.

"You think he doesn't know who we are?" asked Bill Knox.

"I don't know if he was playing us or if he really didn't know, but one thing is for sure. If he didn't know, he's going to be really upset when he finds out I told him a lie."

"Yeah, we need to come ready the next time," Bill Knox said. "We have not seen the last of them."

We made it back to the boat ramp in just a few minutes and it didn't take us long to get the boat loaded. As we loaded and got in the truck to leave, we were discussing the three men. We were still stunned by the fact that we had been approached by the same three men we believed to be the ones that tried to run us off the road.

"I know that is the same three people," I said. "I recognized the one sitting in the back of the boat by his haircut. I remember when they were walking down the road in Texas, and I thought it was a strange haircut. It looks like somebody turned a bowl over his head and went around it with a weed eater."

"It has to be the same people," Bill said. "But it blows my mind that they don't recognize us. I don't believe in coincidences. I think they know who we are and were just testing us."

"Yeah, you're probably right," I agreed. "They could have gotten all the information they needed from Jasper Brown. I'm sure that his daddy told him everything in order to get Jasper to stop beating him. We have to consider them dangerous. They tried to run us off the road, and I'm sure they are the ones that put the rattlesnakes in my mail box."

"Let's hope your gun permit came," said Bill. "I'll bet you a large amount of greenbacks that they're carrying."

We were just pulling into the parking place at my house when my cell phone rang. It was Darwin Brown III. He told me that he had just gotten released from the hospital, but was still having trouble getting around. The beating had been severe. He also told me that Jasper had been offered a deal if he would plead guilty. He said that he had brought charges against Jasper, and so had the boy that Jasper had forced to drive to Texas. I told him about the three guys and he felt sure they were Jasper's friends. He said that the group Jasper had run with had been known to create some havoc when anyone crossed them.

Before we hung up, he also told me that he had talked to the officials in Texas about having DNA tests to see if Jasper was really his son.

"Let me tell you the good thing that came out of this," he said. "My wife left me while I was in the hospital and filed for a divorce. She doesn't want anything, just out of the marriage. I'm going to sell the house and move on with my life. I've got to move some stuff that you know about, but I will get all that done. I feel like a free man."

"What did he have on his mind?' asked Bill.

"He just wanted to let me know that sometimes a good butt-kicking is worth all the pain," I replied.

We decided that it would probably be best if we didn't mention the three guys that we had met at the lake to the ladies. We didn't unhook the boat after we arrived back at my house, and we loaded what tools we thought we would use to begin the digging. I came out of the shed with two short-handled shovels and one long-handled one, and a mattock. Bill suggested that we take the long-handled hoe with us also. I unrolled a six-foot blue tarp and we covered the tools with it. All that was left to do now would be to load our vines that we were going to use for cover, and we would leave those in the barrel until we pulled out for the lake tonight. Bill came out of the shed with a short-handled sledge hammer and some wooden stakes and put them under the tarp.

"What do you plan to do with those rattlesnakes?" he asked. "Those dudes have got a nasty disposition. You get close to that aquarium and they get really irritated."

"I know. It makes it a challenge to feed them," I said.

"What are you feeding them?" Bill asked.

"Rats. No, not rats, mice. I've been feeding them mice. The guy I am buying the mice from told me the snakes can go a long time without drinking water. They get their water from the food they eat. I don't know how I would water them. Squirt it down in there with a hose, I guess. It's dangerous enough just to try and put the mice in there."

"Don't you feel bad dropping those mice in there with those two big rattlesnakes?"

"Not really," I said. "I don't like mice anymore than I like snakes. It's survival of the fittest; they're just part of the food chain."

"Now, my last question for you," Bill said. "What do you plan to do with them?"

"I've got an idea that came to me yesterday," I answered. "I knew I was keeping them for a reason, but I'll just have to see if my plan works. I think the snakes won't be here much longer. It will be a surprise."

We were going to leave to go digging at 9 o'clock. It would be totally dark then. We planned to dig for four hours unless we made a big discovery. We knew we had to leave ourselves enough time after digging to fix the site to where it looked like no one had been there.

After lunch, I was taking a nap to get energized for the night when my cell phone rang. It was Mrs. Ella Knight of the Stoney Point DAR. She wanted me to come to their meeting at noon on Monday to give them an update on the marker. I started to decline, but thought, why not? It might be fun.

I told her that I would be bringing a guest who could help me shed some light on the situation. I also told her that we would not be able to join them until after lunch. She expressed her regrets.

"Mrs. Eugenia Courtney is in charge of preparing the meal, and she always has great surprises," Mrs. Knight said. I didn't doubt her.

At 8:30 we finished loading the boat. We took the vines out of the water and pushed them gently into a five-gallon bucket we were taking in case we found gold coins. Becky and Anita had packed us sandwiches and two thermoses of coffee. During the night I had remembered that I had a metal detector. I could not believe that it had not come to mind before. The last time I had used it was almost three years ago in Florida, where I had found a matchbox car and a penny. I changed the batteries and put it into the boat also. I was beginning to wonder if there was going to be room for us.

The boat ramp we used was also a campground. I surveyed the area when we pulled up, but I didn't see a boat that matched the one the three guys had been in, and although we couldn't be sure what they were driving, I didn't see a maroon van, at least. We launched the boat and headed out at a very slow speed. To go any faster up the lake, I would need to use a bright light to see. I didn't want to hit anything in the water, but I also did not want call attention to us. I cut the engine well before we got to the big flat rock. We each took an oar and slowly moved up the shore line. There was no sign of any other boats on the lake, and there appeared to be no activity around the houses next to the lake.

We moved into the bank where the flat rock was and found a piece of driftwood to tie the boat. I covered the area with the metal detector, but did not receive a hit. I placed it back into the boat and we each took a short-handled shovel and moved to where we had decided to dig.

The soil was loose and the digging was not hard. We had decided to move the soil to one side. Our thinking was that if we dropped the dirt into the lake instead, it would muddy the water and might draw attention to the site. We went at it hard. Moving dirt one shovel full at a time, we soon had a big hole dug. The problem was we had not seen anything that looked like a treasure chest. In fact, we had not even hit anything. We hadn't even found a rock. We took a break, ate a sandwich, and drank some coffee. It was about an hour later that Bill hit something with his shovel. My heart rate increased rapidly when I heard the clank.

"What have you got?" I asked.

"I don't know. I'm trying to adjust my light to see if I can make it out."

I moved over a step or two to try and help. The lights shining from our hats showed plainly a piece of steel, and we dug for about 10 more minutes and recovered it. It did not seem to be anything significant. It was a piece of steel about four feet long and about six inches wide. It had no holes, nor did it look like it had ever been connected to anything. The mystery was how this piece of steel got this far underground.

It was the only thing we hit the rest of the night. We dug for four hours, taking short breaks when we felt the need. One thing we realized was that we had dug deep enough and wide enough to have found a treasure if there had been one there. We would now have to take another approach. We spent the next hour putting dirt back in the hole, and covering the site with the vines that we had brought. We drove stakes in the ground and attached the vines. We would come back later on in the day and see how the digging site looked with the vines draped over it. It was an exhausting night, and there was nothing to show for it.

"Did you ever see that movie *Holes*?" I asked.

"Yeah, I did. I think I remember it," Bill said.

"Remember that little girl out in the desert digging for the treasure with her grandpa?" I asked him. "She said, 'I'm tired, Grandpa,' and he said, 'That's too damn bad, keep digging.' We've just got to keep digging."

"Shit, I thought you were going to tell me something profound," Bill said.

"I'm too tired to even spell profound," I answered.

CHAPTER THIRTEEN

Rattlesnakes are temperamental at 7 in the morning. I was carrying them from the shed to the boat, and they were most unhappy. One was actually striking the inside of the glass. Maybe, like me, they didn't want to get up that early. I felt awful. My arms and shoulders hurt, and the lack of sleep was making me feel groggy. I was just not used too that much physical labor.

Bill admitted that he felt the same. He watched me load the snakes, but did not ask why I was taking them. I went in my garage and when I returned I had a piece of brown paper and some duct tape. I placed the paper around the aquarium that housed the snakes and taped it down securely so that no one would be able to see inside the glass.

We sat in the truck at the boat ramp and finished our coffee and our steak biscuits we had purchased at a fast-food place. It was a beautiful morning. The lake was totally calm. There was no wind, and the water was as smooth as glass. We sipped our coffee and watched a family of mallards swimming in line. The male was in the lead, with the mother and six fuzzy little ones swimming behind him.

"I saw this same scene once right here," I told Bill. "It was still, and about this calm, and all of sudden there was a big splash of water, and one of the little ducklings was gone. I guess a big bass got it. The mother duck went crazy. She was quacking and swimming in circles. The other little ducks got on her back and finally they came ashore." I went on. "I also saw a huge bass take out a red-winged blackbird on Lake

Okeechobee like that one day. The black bird was sitting on a lily pad pecking at something. It wandered close to the edge, and all of a sudden it was history. That bass came out of the water and took the bird right off the pad."

"Sort of like dropping a white mouse in on top of a rattlesnake," Bill said.

"Those rattlesnakes kind of bug you a little bit, I believe."

"I just am amazed you kept them. Most people would have killed them, or at least reported to the police that someone put them inside your mail box. Those two creatures back there in that container are never going to make pets."

"Well, their time is at hand," I told him. "I've got a feeling we won't be hauling them around much longer."

We put the boat in the water, and headed up the lake to the digging site. There were four more empty trailers sitting in the parking area, so there was an excellent chance that the three men could be out there. We had no idea what they were driving. Also, there was a very good possibility that they were launching from a totally different boat ramp.

As we made our way up the lake we did not see any other boats. I shut the engine down in front of where Admiral Farragut's monument used to stand and using the trolling motor to keep us straight. We fished up to the flat rock where we had dug during the night. The vines looked normal hanging there. We had done a very good job of concealing the digging site. Satisfied that we could have not concealed it any better, we decided to call it a day and get some sleep in order to feel like digging later on. Bill was the first to notice a boat approaching from across the lake. It was the three men in the same aluminum john boat.

"You want me to high-tail out of here or do you want to see what they have on their minds?" I asked Bill.

"Let's see what they have to say," Bill replied. "If we have to leave, we know we can outrun them."

Evidently the boat had been up against the east bank on the other side of the lake, and because the sun was so bright we could not see them. They were almost on us before Bill saw them. We sat and waited for them to pull up next to us.

"How are you guys this morning?" I called out in a cheerful voice.

"We're not here to make small talk," the guy sitting in the bow of the boat said. "You lied to us, and now we want some truthful answers."

"What did I lie about?" I asked.

"You lied about where the monument stood. We found out that that's a different ferry you took us to yesterday."

"That's where I thought it was," I said.

It was then that the man displayed the gun. He came up with the weapon and pointed it straight at me.

"We know you're looking for gold. You might have already found it. But you'd better start telling the truth. I didn't come all the way here to listen to a bunch of your lies. So what's it going to be," he said, waving the gun.

"We have found some gold," I told him. "We haven't found the big haul yet but I have some gold coins here in the boat. I will give them to you. It's all we have. You have to believe that."

I reached down in the boat and came up with the glass container with the snakes. I pretended that it was very heavy. I strained as I picked it up.

"Here are all the gold coins we have. Put down that gun and I'll let you have them," I said.

"I'm not putting down the gun," the man said. "Hand over the coins."

I did just as he asked. Only I didn't hand the container over. I threw it into the bottom of their boat. There was a loud crash when the glass hit the aluminum boat. It took a couple of seconds for it to register to the men in the boat that they were now in the company of some angry rattlesnakes.

The guy with the bad haircut went from the middle of the boat to the back and out into the water. The man in the back went over the side. The one wielding the gun begin firing at the snakes in the bottom of the boat. One of the men in the water yelled at him.

"Hey, dumb ass, you're shooting holes in the bottom of the boat."

The man emptied the gun. Evidently his aim was not all that good, because one of the snakes was moving toward him. He clicked the trigger on the empty gun and then went over the bow into the water.

I grabbed a rope tied to an eyelet on their boat. I started my boat and we left them floundering in the water as I pulled their boat away. We went back by the old ferry and across a cove to the shore. We beached our boat, and I jumped out and started pulling the other boat upon the bank. Once I had it up there, I got the long-handled hoe out of my boat and went looking for the snakes. The boat had been taking water and the snakes had gotten wet, whether they wanted to or not.

They both were highly agitated and were not easy to get out of the boat and onto the ground. I got one out and when he stretched out to get away, I took off his head with one swing of the hoe. The second snake died the same awful death.

I took the shovel out of the boat and dug a deep hole. I scooped up the heads and dropped them in the hole and covered them over with the dirt, as it was my understanding that they could still bite with their heads separated from their bodies. I picked up one of the snake's bodies and threw it into the men's boat, and then I threw the other snake in after the first.

Bill had not moved, he had stood and watched the entire thing unfold. I got back into my boat and waited for Bill to get in and take a seat.

"You are one strange guy," said Bill. "I think that's why I like to hang around with you."

We had loaded the boat and were in the truck headed home before Bill spoke again.

"Do you believe in miracles?" Bill asked.

"Yeah, I do," I said. "What makes you ask that?"

"Well, I think we witnessed one back there when you threw the snakes into the boat," he said.

"You mean because the man shot at the snakes instead of us?" I asked him.

"No, it was when the guy with the weed-eater haircut jumped out of the boat. His next three steps were on top of the water."

CHAPTER FOURTEEN

Driving up the highway home, I was still laughing at Bill's joke, but it was becoming quite clear that this was no laughing matter. The three men were serious about the gold, and we had had too many encounters with them already. Somebody was going to get hurt if we didn't come up with a way to deal with this situation.

Our other topic of discussion was where we were going to dig when we went back later that night. We had dug on both sides of the flat rock, so the next logical place would be under the rock. Bill thought we should start under the rock closer to where the Cherokee brave was found. His theory was that the people who buried the gold would have been in a hurry after the encounter with the Cherokees, and they would have not moved too far.

It had not been a restful sleep. My sleeping habits had been turned upside down, and what little rest I had gotten had been interrupted by dreams of rattlesnakes. In the dream every time I chopped one of the snake's head off, it would grow another head and then turn into another snake. They were multiplying faster than I could keep up with them. The ground was covered with them. I awoke with my heart beating so fast and loud that I could hear it. My shoulders still hurt and my arms still felt like lead. I was going to have to loosen up before tonight. I planned to dig hard and dig deep.

If we found it, the idea was to get the gold hidden as quickly as possible. We would have to save the dirt and fill back in where we dug, because if we put vines there it would not look natural. I had the feeling we were close. The longer we left the gold unfound, the more opportunities it gave someone else to find it. I didn't know what happened to the three guys after we left them yesterday, but I did expect that they would show up again. Maybe it was a sign, because in the mail was my gun permit. I thought it probably wouldn't hurt to take it with me tonight.

Just after dinner I got a call from Darwin Brown III. He wanted to tell me that Jasper was going to plead guilty and not stand trial. It said that he and the young man that Jasper had forced to drive the car had agreed to drop their charges back in Kansas so that the authorities in Texas could get on with the sentencing. Jasper's lawyer had already objected to the DNA test, saying it violated Jasper's rights.

Darwin was having his lawyer work on the matter. I asked him about the three men again, and he said that none of Jasper's crowd seemed capable of big things, and that it was rare for one of them to be involved in a violent, premeditated crime. I told him that when you were looking down a gun barrel, it didn't matter if the guy holding the gun was a hard-time criminal or a petty thief. The gun looked the same.

"I don't think you could take a tornado and blow that bunch Jasper hung around with on anybody," Darwin Brown III said.

"We're not in Kansas anymore, Toto," I replied.

Once again the water was silky smooth and the sky was clear as we launched and made our way up the lake to the digging site. The night was really hot and there was no air stirring. The wind whipping by as we made it up the lake felt good to the skin. The weather forecast was calling for heavy storms for the next two days so we needed to make a lot of progress tonight. It would be really hard to stand on that sloped bank under that rock and dig if it was wet. There was no sign of any other boaters and we cruised into our spot and tied off the boat. We sat for a few minutes, letting our eyes adjust to the darkness. We had decided that one of us would be on watch while the other one dug, looking out especially for those three men, and every hour we would change places. It would go faster if both of us could dig, but we didn't need to be surprised, especially if at least one of them was carrying a gun.

Bill took the first watch and I started the dig. I moved over just under the flat rock that hung out over the lake. The soil was loose and sandy and the digging was easy. Almost at the end of my hour, I hit something with my shovel. I scraped the dirt from around it and dragged it toward me. I know I stopped breathing. It was a gold bar.

I picked it up and was surprised how heavy it was. I had not said anything to Bill when I was uncovering it, so I yelled softly to him to come and look. He couldn't believe his eyes. We started jumping around like two insane people, realizing that we needed to be as quiet as possible but wanting to celebrate this remarkable find.

"So that is a gold bar" is all Bill said.

"Solid gold; there's a lot of money in this little bar here," I said. "I believe this is the first of a lot more to come."

Bill immediately was ready to take his turn at digging. I took a seat in the boat. It was dark out there on that water. Someone could be right on top of you before you ever saw them. It would probably in our best interest to find some night vision goggles before we came back. I had just gotten comfortable when Bill called to me. He had found another bar. We washed it off in the lake and held it under the light. It was a brilliant color, the color of money.

We each took another turn digging and neither of us found anything else. It made no sense. Why would there be two gold bars in there, and no other gold around them? We finally gave up and began trying to make the digging site look as natural as we could. It had really clouded over during the time we had been out there on the lake. It looked for sure like a storm would be moving in. If we could get it covered, we would let the rain settle the dirt back down.

We headed back to load our boat with mixed emotions. We couldn't be happier about the fact that we found two gold bars, but we were baffled that we didn't find more.

"It's a strange feeling," Bill said. "It's kind of happy and sad."

"It's like that old joke," I said. "The one where the guy watches his mother-in-law drive his Bentley off a cliff."

"I don't have a mother-in-law," Bill replied.

"You just came into some extra money. You could buy yourself one," I said.

CHAPTER FIFTEEN

I woke up Sunday morning to the sound of heavy rain, and the smell of a good country breakfast. My wife was cooking bacon, sausage, eggs, milk gravy and homemade cat-eye biscuits. She had already finished a pan of sweet rolls and iced them with a butter-cream orange frosting that was some kind of good. I was enjoying my coffee and starting my second one when she came and moved them out of my reach.

"Anita and Bill are coming to eat with us this morning," she said. "If you fill up on sweet rolls you're not going to want any breakfast. You would be a big help if you would set the dining room table for me."

I had just placed the first plate when the doorbell rang. I went to the door expecting to see Bill and Anita, and was totally surprised to see Jack Winston.

"Come in here out of the rain." I said to Jack. "I didn't expect to see you today."

"I told you I would drop by. I have a meeting in Gatlinburg later this morning with the man that I hope is going to help us."

He came on into the kitchen where Becky was cooking. She was surprised, but glad to see him. They embraced and made small talk for a while. I was sure she was dying to ask him about Linda, but she never did. He accepted a cup of coffee but said that he could not stay for breakfast because of his appointment. I refilled my cup, stirred in a couple of artificial sweeteners and we went into the den to talk.

"Have you found the gold?" he asked. "That is the first question Mr. Big is going to ask me today."

"We have the gold and it is in a safe place," I answered, figuring that if I had two gold bars and they were locked up in my truck, I wasn't really telling him a lie. Then again maybe I was.

"Good, do you know how much?" Jack asked.

I assumed that I should follow one lie with another. "It's a lot. We're going to be rich."

My reasoning for telling him that was if I told him we only had two bars he was not going to push too hard to get his contact to help us. Jack seemed to be very hesitant about the meeting coming up later, and I questioned him about it. He said that he had to be cautious because he had to make sure he could trust his contact. He had to feel his way through it. He was afraid that the man could hold him hostage for his part of the gold, and he knew what he was doing was illegal.

We also discussed the three men that we had encountered. His advice was to treat them as dangerous if they had pulled a gun on us. He could not believe that someone, maybe those three men, had put two rattlesnakes in my mailbox. He declined an invitation to spend the night, saying that his plane was leaving at four and that he had to be back at work in the morning.

"I'll call you when I get to the airport this afternoon and let you know how this meeting went," said Jack. A clap of thunder sounded and he waited until it faded in the distance before continuing.

"Surely you're not going to hunt gold in this kind of weather," he said.

"No," I answered. "It's supposed to be like this all the way through tomorrow. I think we'll stay in until all of this blows out of here."

Bill and Anita were arriving at the door just as I was saying goodbye to Jack. They exchanged pleasantries and Jack was gone. It was clear that Jack was a long way away from being warmed up to Bill Knox. You could see it in his body demeanor. There was something about Bill that Jack didn't like or didn't trust. Bill had never commented on Jack one way or another, nor did his eyes or facial expressions give any indication as to how he felt. I had known Jack Winston for a long time and had had no problem trusting his instincts. This time, however, I thought he might be wrong. Bill Knox was a square-dealing, straight-shooting kind of guy. I trusted him wholeheartedly.

We were sitting at the breakfast table when Anita held at her hand for us to see. On her finger was an engagement ring.

"Bill and I want to get married tomorrow if we can," she said.

"Tomorrow," Becky said. "It might not be possible to find anybody to marry you by tomorrow."

"Surely there is a Justice of the Peace that would do this," said Anita. "We want you two to stand up for us."

"Well, I'll tell you what," I said to Becky. "You and Anita find a JP, and when Bill and I get back from our little engagement with the DAR, we'll go get this thing done."

Monday morning the rain was still falling heavily. There was water standing where I hadn't seen water before. I was getting restless. I had spent Sunday reading, and had even taken a nap, but I needed to get back to digging for the gold. Sunday night Jack Winston had called me from the airport, and said that the meeting went well with his contact. Jack felt the man could be trusted, and he told him that he would be in touch when we were ready to move the gold.

We were going to have to go tonight and resume digging if at all possible. Waiting one more day seemed too long to me. Too many things could happen. We had no idea what the digging site looked like after all this rain. It would be muddy and the dirt would be heavy, but we would just have to find a way to get it done. My biggest concern was that the three men had either repaired their boat or gotten another boat, and had also found the site.

Bill and I arrived at the Lowe's Ferry Methodist Church just after the members of the Daughters of the American Revolution had finished eating. I was certainly glad of that.

"You are welcome to eat if you like," said Mrs. Knight.

"Thank you very much," I replied. "We had a late breakfast and we have early dinner plans."

"You are missing a real treat," Mrs. Knight told me. "We had Mrs. Courtney's ham salad molded into the shape of a lamb and served with mint jelly. Our vegetable was steamed acorn squash. Our dessert was coconut milk with graham crackers."

I would have slit my throat with a rusty butter knife before I would have tried any of that.

Our presentation to the members was brief and concise. Yes, we told them, we had located the marker. It was in very good condition, but the current owner had no intention of handing it over. I told the group that we were trying very hard to get it back without having to pay any compensation. We left them with assurance that we would be back to discuss this matter with them again. We said our goodbyes and shook hands all the way around. The Regent Miss Hancock sat motionless in her lift chair with a smile plastered on her face. I told Bill later that I thought the mint jelly had stuck her upper lip to her dentures.

"You attract some weird people," Bill said. "I've only known you a short time and already I am seeing a pattern. Has it always been this way?" he asked.

"Pretty much my whole life," I replied.

He shook his head, and muttered. "Damn, a ham lamb."

CHAPTER SIXTEEN

Bill Knox spent his wedding night on a clay embankment under a flat rock looking for a treasure chest supposedly left there more than 200 years before. The wedding had been a very short ceremony. The no- nonsense Justice of the Peace appeared to have more pressing issues. She took care of the paperwork and performed the rites in less than 10 minutes.

Now here Bill was, trying to keep the red clay mud from sticking to his shovel. It was back-breaking work. Trying to stand on the wet slope and move heavy scoops of dirt was tiring us both out very quickly. Again the metal detector had failed to give us a ping and I wondered if the thing still worked. I was sure the gold was in this location. Why would there be two gold bars in this spot and nothing else? We each would take a turn digging and then have to rest.

It was getting late, and Bill was taking his last turn before we quit for the night, when his shovel struck something solid. We could not tell what it was but in my mind it was the treasure chest. We both crowded in close so the lights on our hats could illuminate the area. It was a solid piece of wood, but there was not any clue as to what it was. I jabbed my shovel toward one end of the wooden piece, trying to locate where it ended. Bill was jabbing at the other end. It was getting late and we had to make a decision what we were going to do.

Actually the decision was easy. As hard as it was to walk away from what we thought was the treasure, we could not dig during the daylight hours. We were going to have to cover the site over and once again make it look like no one had been there. Covering it up and making it secure was as hard as uncovering it. We were exhausted when we finally finished. We sat down on the seats of the boat and changed in to other shoes that we had brought. The boots we were wearing were covered with red clay mud. One more day of hard digging and I was sure that the treasure would be ours. We headed down the lake to the landing site as happy as we could be.

Remember Robert Burns the poet telling the mouse that sometimes the best laid plans go awry, and leave us nothing but grief and pain? Bill and I were not strangers to grief and pain. In fact, it seemed to be just around the corner waiting on us. We arrived at the boat ramp around three in the morning and there were only two cars there. There was a tent pitched on the far edge away from the ramp, and there were no boat trailers. It appeared that Bill and I were the only ones out on the lake. I backed the truck down to the ramp and put the trailer into the water. Bill drove the boat onto the trailer and I pulled it out of the water.

We were strapping the boat to the trailer with the winch and the tie-downs when we realized we had company. It wasn't three this time, but four. Out of the shadows came two men on the right side of the boat and two on the left side. One of the men on the right had a gun and one of the men on the left had a gun. We must have been tired, or lulled to security by the inactivity in the campground. We never saw them until it was too late. They all had on black pants, black shirts, and black ski masks pulled over their heads. The gunman on the right side was first to speak. He waved the gun erratically and pointed it straight at me.

"This is your last chance to get this right," the guy said to me. "I'm tired of your smart-ass ways. You might have thought leading us to the wrong spot and throwing rattlesnakes in our boat made you the winner, but the time has come to pay up. You are going to take us to the gold or I'm going to shoot both of you. So now is the time to decide."

"I don't have any gold," I replied. "We haven't found it yet."

"Don't lie to me," the guy said. "We know you have gold. You've got a half an hour to get us to where you've got it stored."

The other men stood there, one of them with his gun pointed at us also, and never talked. The one who was doing the talking I recognized as the one that had shot at the snakes in the boat. I decided to try and see if I could rile him. I pointed to the man standing by the gunman's side.

"I am surprised to see you still with this guy," I said. "You watched him shoot holes in your boat and you come back with him."

"You're wasting time," the talker said. "You better get us to where the gold is. Your time is running out."

"There is no way to get to where the gold is in less than a half an hour," I said, making up a story as I went. "It will take at least an hour, and I am stopping up the road here and going thru the drive-thru for a cup of coffee. You can get one or wait I don't really care."

The right-side gunman motioned to the man on the left holding the gun.

"You get in the truck with them," he said to the man. "If he has not got us to the gold in an hour, stop them and if you don't shoot them I will. I'll allow the coffee. I could use a cup myself."

The man climbed into the back of my dual cab and motioned with his gun for us to get in. He still had not uttered a word. I had the strangest feeling that I had met him somewhere before, but I couldn't place him.

"You think you can talk now that your brave leader is in the other car?" I asked the man.

He didn't speak, just waved the gun at me, and I started the truck and pulled out of the campground. There was no conversation at all as we went up the highway. I could see that the other car was staying up with me, and I knew sooner or later Bill and I were going to have to come up with a plan. Bill sat on the passenger side and stared out of the window. You could almost hear the wheels turning in his head. I pulled into the fast food drive-thru and watched as the car following me made its turn also. I was still trying to place the person sitting in the back seat of my truck. I pulled up to the speaker and waited for the person inside to ask for my order. She came on and asked my order.

"I want three regular cups of coffee, please," I said. "I want one black, one with two packs of Sweet-and-Low, and one with two packs of sugar. You still take two sugars in your coffee don't you?" I asked the man in the back who was holding the gun.

"Yeah, two sugars," he replied.

"You bastard, I knew it was you," I said.

Jack Winston ripped the ski mask off and waved the gun at me. "I need that gold and I need it bad. Those guys back there following us are never going to get it. I hate that it had to come to this, but I am in big trouble and I need that gold now. So you can forget about those clowns back there. It's me you are dealing with now."

I pulled my truck around to the fast food window, handed the woman my money, and waited for my change and the coffees. I pulled the truck and the boat off to the side and waited for the three men behind us to get their order. I stirred the artificial sugar into my coffee and put two sugars into the other cup and handed it to Jack Winston.

"I didn't figure you could hold a gun on me and stir your coffee," I said. "Look, the truth is, Jack, we don't have any gold. We have found two bars. They are laying right here on the console." I picked one up and gestured with it as I talked. "We've been digging for quite some time but we don't have it yet. I told you we had gold so you would go on with the deal you were making in Gatlinburg. I figured if I told you we didn't have the gold yet you wouldn't find a way to exchange it. For the last time, we don't have the gold."

"Don't lie to me," Jack yelled. "I have to have this gold. I am running now to keep from getting killed. I owe huge gambling debts, and the people I owe want their money. I'm not leaving here without that gold."

"I fully intended to give you a share of the money for helping us with the disposition of it. I told you that."

"You don't understand," he said. "I've lost my wife, I've lost my job, I've lost all my friends, and I'm going to lose my life if I don't come up with some money, lots of money."

"You can count me in that bunch of friends you lost. Most of my friends don't hold guns on me," I said.

Jack looked back toward the drive-thru. "What's taking that bunch of idiots so long? They must have ordered breakfast. I want you to know that I am not kidding about this. Bad things are going to happen if you don't take me to that gold."

It happened quickly. Bill shifted in his seat, put the coffee cup to his lips as if to take a sip, and all in one motion threw the entire hot contents into Jack Winston's face. Jack screamed in pain, dropped the gun and grabbed his face. With one quick move, I went up the side of Jack's head with the gold bar. He went down onto the seat and never moved. It was so smooth it was like Bill and I had practiced before-hand.

"There's an old Eskimo saying that says you never can tell your friends from your enemies until the ice breaks," I said to Bill. "I guess the ice just broke."

"I might have melted it with that cup of hot coffee," Bill panned.

CHAPTER SEVENTEEN

It was 7:30 in the morning before Bill and I got away from the police station and made it back home. We had called our wives and told them the story. Bill dialed 911 while Jack Winston lay knocked out cold on the back seat, and the three stooges behind us ate their breakfast. Bill had told the dispatcher that in addition to the police he needed an ambulance, because he felt for sure that Jack Winston had serious burns and could have a concussion or a fractured skull.

We were on our way toward the police station with the other men following us when the blue lights and sirens overtook us. The three men who had been following us were arrested without incident. In fact they gave up rather peacefully. It was at the police station that things got really confused. The other man who had the gun was named Richard Roberts, and he had several stories to tell the police. He admitted putting rattlesnakes in my mailbox, and told the police that I had tossed them back into their boat. He admitted that he and his two friends had kidnapped Anita Walsh, and that they had tried to run us off the road in Texas.

Jack Winston was in with them, according to Roberts, at least since he had met them after they had run us off the road. Their motive for everything that they had done was because I had stolen gold from their friend Jasper Brown. According to Roberts, Jack Winston had believed there was gold, and that I knew where it was located. For what seemed like the one hundredth time I told the story about thinking there could have been gold in the marker. I also spent a great deal of time telling the detective in charge about Jack Winston. I had been totally betrayed by a man I had known for a lot of years. Just before we left the police station I was told that Jack would be in the hospital for a time, but was expected to recover. When he was dismissed from the hospital he would be arrested.

Bill and I did not go back and dig for gold that night. As much as we could hear it calling us, we were too tired to answer. The next night, however, we were rearing to go. There was not anyone around when we launched our boat and we did not see anyone on the lake as we made our way to where we were sure there was treasure. We tied the boat to our usual piece of driftwood, and I took a shovel and my metal detector with me to the site. After I had finished digging out the dirt we had used to camouflage the area, I turned on the metal detector and ran it next to the piece of wood we had found before. There was a distinct ping. It could be some kind of rusty old steel, but my heart was singing gold.

It took three swings with the pick to break away the wood, and then we saw it. There was gold, thousands of gold coins shinning as bright as the sun, under the lights that gleamed from our hats.

Bill and I stared at it in silence for a few minutes.

"Don't you have anything profound to say?" he asked.

"Holy Miss Hancock," I said.

EPILOGUE

The hurricane was still miles out to sea, but we had decided today was the day we needed to leave the island. We were loading the plane with only essential papers and keepsakes, including the nice collection of scarce first edition mysteries I had picked up from Anita Walsh Knox. If the storm held its course, there was a good possibility that the island that we were living on could be washed away. If that was the end result, then Bill Knox and I would have to find another one to buy. I suppose that's what you do when you have as much gold as we have. It would be hard to find a better place to live. The scenery was great, as was the fishing. Our wives loved the place, and never tired of painting the sunsets and seascapes.

We finished loading, took one look around, and soon were airborne. Our first stop would be in Kansas, because we needed to talk to Darwin Brown III, who had turned the gold we had found into a valuable asset for Bill and me and our wives. Darwin had agreed to take care of the gold, keeping it in a secluded place, and getting it converted to cash. He turned out to be the logical choice, since for a man who already had all the gold he needed; he had the least case of gold rush fever than anyone I'd ever seen.

It had taken us over a month to move all the gold from where we found it. We have not and do not want to count all the gold coins that were buried at that flat rock. It had been back-breaking work, but we had completed it, and were rich beyond our wildest dreams. We had not kept all the riches to ourselves. We had seen that others were taken care of, especially those closest to us. One of the things we had done over the Christmas season was to fly to different towns and drop gold coins into the Salvation Army kettles. It just seemed to be a way to do some good.

My last stop on this trip from the island would be in Knoxville. I had promised Mrs. Ella Knight that I would update the Stoney Point chapter of the DAR on the Farragut marker. I also wanted to get updated on Jack Winston and his three helpers. Rumor had it that they had received stiff sentences, but I wanted to be sure. I didn't want to be looking over my shoulder.

I met Mrs. Knight at the door of the meeting room and was invited inside. She seated me at the speakers' table and said lunch would be served in just a few moments. I noticed that Miss Hancock was sitting at her usual place in her lift chair. Lunch was unique to say the least. Actually I didn't think it was too bad. That is if you like beet salad with goat cheese. Dessert was sauerkraut cupcakes with cream frosting. The punch was fresh mango with pulp, diluted with guava nectar.

Different ladies introduced different business issues and these were discussed and voted on. I finished my salad while they tended to business. I had just finished my cupcake and drained my punch cup when Mrs. Knight introduced me as the speaker.

"Good afternoon ladies. Your entertainment director, Mrs. Knight, has asked me back to give you an update on the marker or monument of Admiral David Farragut. The last I heard the monument had been located and negotiations were underway to return it. I hope that is true, because, ladies, I have already spent too much of my time and my money hunting that piece of rock.

"I have wasted energy and resources hunting something that nobody gave a gray rat's butt about until it was gone. My question is, why do you care anyway? You want the marker to be found because Admiral Farragut's father fought in the Revolutionary War. You ladies are treating Jorge Farragut as a hero, but I am here to tell you he was a soldier of fortune, interested in his own selfish gains. He left a pregnant wife with small children in an Indian-infested wilderness to go off on another self-gratifying journey. Leaving her to load the livestock and belongings and sail to New Orleans. The woman was five months with child and the trip took two months.

"You're honoring a man as a hero who gave David Farragut up for adoption when the boy was 8 years old. He fought in the War of 1812 when he was 11. History says that Jorge Farragut's wife died of yellow fever. However, the only outbreak of yellow fever that year was in Philadelphia. I propose to you that she died from a sexually transmitted disease, as result of Jorge Farragut's philandering.

"In conclusion, ladies, I'm over it. I don't care anymore about the marker. I feel like I've been sent for and couldn't go. Shot at and missed and shit at and hit. Here is my recommendation: Get up off of your bony regal historical revolution backsides and bring it back yourselves."

I stepped off the speaker platform and headed for the door. As I exited I noticed that the members had gathered around the chair of Mrs. Hancock. She was lying back in the chair and one of the ladies was fanning her. I caught Mrs. Knight's attention.

"Cancel my tickets to this circus," I said. "I've seen this act before."

Made in the USA
Charleston, SC
24 February 2012